JUNIPER LEAVES
The Otherworldly Tale of a Lonesome Magical Girl

NPL F

Nashville Public Library | FOUNDATION

D1372991

Jaz Joyner

b l a c k p a n s y

An Imprint of Black Pansy Books

New York, New York

Copyright © 2017 Jasper Joyner.

ISBN-paperback: 978-0-9995386-1-6
ISBN-hardcover: 978-0-9995386-2-3
ISBN-ebook: 978-0-9995386-0-9

Original Cover Design by Michael Bennett and Jalisa Joyner
Inspired by Aspen Aten

Manufactured in the USA

To those of you who told me I better not give up on this thing.
You know who you are.

Jaz Joyner

CHAPTER ONE

I USED TO WANT TO BE a magician. Now this was long before I took my first science class, and if I'm being really real, before I found out what real-life magicians actually were. As far as my five-year-old brain was concerned, magicians had the secrets to life, and everyone else was just not fantastic enough to figure it out. Juxtapose that with my dad, a scientist and avid *National Geographic* reader with twice as many space-themed vests as Neil deGrasse Tyson. I may not talk much, but I never shied away from a debate with the Mick himself. Mick is the nickname my dad has people call him, because, yes, he's the kind of guy that creates his own nicknames.

One time, I really thought I had him. I was seven and sitting on his lap while he read Nat Geo and smacked on sunflower seeds, a snack he tells me he eats to keep from smoking. That day, he was looking at pictures of beautiful green, blue and yellow lights just hovering over evergreen trees.

I pointed, my eyes wide with innocence, "Look, Dad. I told you there's magic!"

I was quite confident in my assessment and tilted my head at him as if I'd just won a game of chess.

He laughed and said, "Ah, Junebug, that's actually called Aurora Borealis. It's no more than a natural effect that occurs when the Earth experiences something called geomagnetic storms..."

I'm going to stop there, because that's when I totally zoned out. *Do you actually think I'm interested in a science lesson at this very moment when I've proven magic?* It's like he was incapable of thinking outside of the box, or at least that's what my seven-year-old mind thought. Don't get me wrong, science is my favorite subject in school, and it's fun and all, but back then, I didn't feel like science and magic could exist in the same world. Science was the enemy, the rain on my parade, the apple to my orange in a universe where oranges are the only relevant fruit.

Over the years, I held on tight to fantasies despite Dad's attempts to bring me back to reality. But then, by no fault of my dad's, I stopped believing in everything, just like that. Well, not just like that — some pretty fucked up things happened in between — but I'll tell you that later. Also, I kinda love that I can write "fuck" and not get in trouble for it, but I've actually never said it out loud. I feel you should know that about me, and I ask that you don't judge. Or do. It's cool (it's not cool, I'm embarrassed). Anyway, I was fifteen, and life gave me just enough reason to give up on magic, until a summer in North Carolina that turned my whole world upside-down.

Do you know what happens when you sit in the middle of a Chevrolet Express for more than five hours? I do. You space out. You forget you're a fully functioning human with a brain and get lost in the sky outside your window. I squinted hard at the slow-moving clouds, one hand shielding my eyes, and the other hanging out the window, bouncing along with the ride. I gazed up at a lion with a ferocious mane and imagined it was looking to pounce. As was I. I was pissed with no place to channel my anger, and the clouds knew it. I could tell.

The van rumbled and rolled over rocky southern roads on the path to North Carolina, every inch making me more homesick than the next.

"About two more hours!" The driver shouted in a thick accent I couldn't quite place, his flesh-colored beard misty with sweat.

He looked like an extra from *The Lord of the Rings* with his white-blonde hair and arms the same size as tires are round. He's a scientist too. A scientist with a van large enough for my dad's equipment and kind enough to let us borrow it for three months, if only we let him ride with us to North Carolina so he could see his old "sweetheart." My dad didn't dare delve into the backstory on that, but till this day, I'm curious who Broadie, the driver, went to see.

I tried doodling in my journal as the van rolled on the craggy road, but, I assure you, there's no such thing as quality journaling in a vehicle controlled by Thor. So back to the clouds I went. I always wondered what kids with siblings would do at times like these. Like, would you actually talk to each other? Would you play a game, or laugh about whatever odd thing your parents are doing?

I'm basically an only child, but only in that I have no siblings around my age. I have a brother who's fifteen years older than me, and apparently I was a "miracle baby surprise." I never see my brother, since he's got a newborn and lives across the country in Palo Alto, California. He's pretty cool, though. He opted out on the North Carolina trip on account of having a life, but unfortunately since I have none, I was required to go. Mom tried giving me her best pitch over the past few weeks as to why I should be excited.

"Just imagine! It's full of hills and nature and space for you to roam. And the McKinneys' farm has a beautiful garden like you like."

And then she did the thing where she'd clasp her hands together, and her eyes would brighten as if she was casting a spell for joy. It didn't work.

"I don't care about gardens anymore, Mom," I lied.

Gardens are awesome, but only sometimes and only in some ways. Like if we were going to some cool city like Charlotte to work on a community garden with a bunch of locals. Or, if we were working on a garden full of newly discovered plants that we'd get to study later in a lab. But no, we were headed to Evershire, a remote, boondock town far outside all things worthy of my time, to work on a farm that just so happened to have a garden in it.

Of course my dad was still excited, though. He'd spent years and years around plants all for the chance to do what this trip would allow, so I don't blame him. My dad is such a nerd he even took off time from "the dating scene" to continue his studies. My parents didn't even meet till their thirties, and my mom didn't have me till she turned forty-five. They may be old, but sometimes I feel like my dad has more energy than the guys at my school. I still worry about them peacing out on me before I'm old enough to not need them anymore. And by that I mean I hope they never die. It's something I don't let myself think about, but I'd be lying to you if I didn't at least mention it. It freaks me out and it crosses my mind more than I'm going to admit. If it were up to me, I'd prefer they just become cyborgs and be alive forever. It's making me twitch as I write this, so let's just talk about Evershire again, cool?

There wasn't much in Evershire's isolation that appealed to me. Rural places rarely do. Maybe it's because I'm already from a small college town but I always wanted to live in a popular city. I want to hear horns honking while I try to sleep and be surrounded by hundreds of people on my daily walk to school. I want to feel like I'm a part of something big, important, something perfectly chaotic and beautifully intricate, like a complicated puzzle. Cut to obsolete, insignificant Evershire, the land of the boring and simple and oddly refined. But it was beautiful . . . Out the window of that Chevrolet were majestic, brown cows in a pasture of fresh green grass that looked like it had been strategically painted one blade at a time. I'd never seen brown cows before, only black and white ones, like in all those "Stop Eating Animals!" sort of documentaries.

I opened my window a bit more, and the humidity punched me in the face like a fart. I clung to a lone crimp, and my tight black curls poofed in the air. I played with it, because what else was I going to do as gravity disappeared for a few seconds, while we flew over a steep hill in a death van. It was like I could fly into space if my seat belt weren't holding me down. *That'd be cool,* I thought.

Dad sat in front of me beside Broadie, the back of his shaved head just barely peeking over the seat as he turned to smile at me. My dad's a little guy, only a few inches taller than me, but you wouldn't know it talking to him. You know how some people have big personalities? Well, my dad has a tall one. Everything he does is elevated and lofty, stretched, even long-winded. When he really gets going, Dad's like a giant sequoia that can't help but catch people's attention. Out of boredom, I tuned in to the tail end of Dad and Broadie's conversation.

Dad cleared his throat, "Did I ever end up telling you about the Valeferus? Have you heard of it?"

My dad knows no one had heard of the Valeferus, because he was the one who'd named it. So of course Broadie shook his head,

"No, I can't say I have."

I could just feel my dad's mouth curl into the proudest smile as he said, "Well, it's a little plant that packs a punch. I believe it's going to lead to great discoveries..."

Dad's a professor, and the reason my whole family made the trek hundreds of miles south. His university funded the trip so he could continue research on a rare plant native to the Carolinian wetlands, the Valeferus. He had strong evidence linking elements of the Valeferus to a possible cure for a rare autoimmune disease his late brother had. For him, this wasn't just a science project: it was his passion. It took years to get the funding, so when the board finally approved, he was over the moon. Honestly, we all were — especially Mom. She knew how much it meant to him, how hard and how long he'd been working at it.

Speaking of my mom, I haven't said much about her yet. You probably noticed. I just want you to know that I know that. She sat beside me in the back of the van, quiet and stoic like a statue. She hadn't spoken more than ten words the whole ride, which, at six hours in, was *very* unlike her. On most days, my parents are bouncing ideas off each other, both equally energetic and excited, "high on life" types. Mom's a nutritionist and fitness instructor, and the sort of person who finds any reason to move around. She always has something to say, but not just for the sake of speaking. No, she'd make sure to have a story, or a fun fact she'd learned, or a cute quote she remembered from her morning reading that she'd use to prompt discussion. But this day was different. This particular trip was meant for "strict relaxation." Her words, not mine, though relaxed is the last thing that would come to mind for anyone looking at her in that moment.

She looked at me, and despite her smile, the pain behind her eyes was palpable. I couldn't look at her anymore. As against this trip as I was, as furious as I was bopping around in that silly van, Mom should have been even more, because it was her mother, my grandmother, who had just died. Her soul sister and my best friend. She was supposed to be in that van with us, beside me, talking to me and laughing with me. I stared back out the window like the answer to my escape was out there.

What was that? I shook my head, as I tried dismissing the image from my mind. That did nothing. I was seeing things. I was legit out of my mind. It couldn't be real. The thought of me momentarily losing it felt more likely than believing. I sat back and tried to relax. I was tightly wound, and clearly there was no stopping that.

Mom was massaging her temples, the edges of her teeny-weeny afro beaded with sweat. She was tense, tapping her finger on her thigh like she was keeping some internal rhythm in her head. It physically hurt me to look at her, and when she caught my gaze, it was obvious I had the same effect. It's not that I was surprised, since Grandma had died only six weeks ago. But the fact that she agreed to this trip at all, so soon, frustrated me. I hadn't forgiven her for that.

We passed a stream between the grass, and it glistened like silver. Light flickered around the water like little fairies fluttering, and as we rolled away, they lingered behind, as if deliberately following. The light bounced past my view and floated in front of me. I shut my eyes and shook my head, only to find the light still there and clearer than before. It had a serene face and what looked like a human body, and it hovered, looking at me. I froze in my seat.

"Almost there!" Broadie shouted.

What. The. Hell. My eyes darted to Broadie and then back, but the figure was gone. I took a breath to calm myself and rolled down the window even more. Mist relieved my clammy brown skin, but couldn't keep my mind from racing. My eyes watered, and I sneezed, my relentless allergies bringing me back to reality.

The night before we left our home in Hamilton, New York, I dreamed Grandma was still alive. That she would meet us at the gas station where we'd leave for North Carolina in the morning and get right in the van with me.

She'd tell Broadie to put the radio on some classics. She'd start a sing-along, and my mom and dad would belt with her to songs I didn't know.

But that morning, as I waved goodbye to my hometown, my much older brother and his family seeing us off, I had to remind myself she wouldn't be joining me. I cried the first two hours before running out of tears, and all the while I fumed at that empty seat next to me. We would have played "I Spy," like we did on our summer trips to Cape Cod. Grandma knew I preferred body language over spoken word, and she would have asked me how I was doing in the sign language we'd made up.

Still, I sat alone, hundreds of miles from anything that kept me close to her. And magic? Please. That was the farthest thing from my mind. It was Grandma's stories that kept me believing in magic for as long as I did. I was the thirteen-year-old kid who cries when their classmates reveal there's no Santa Claus. Not because of my parents but because of Grandma, who simply told me whatever I believe could be real, can be. Nobody could tell me magic wasn't real, and I know that sounds ridiculous now, but when Grandma was alive, it made all the sense in the world.

Grandma once told me a story of a juniper field a few miles back at her childhood home. It was so far from the rest of the farm that she'd wake up in the early hours of the morning, just so she could have time to get back there and play alone before her seven other siblings would make their way over. She told me about figures the size of dragonflies, with wings and tiny human faces. They ate juniper buds and only came out when she was very, very quiet. I used to search for those creatures when I was younger, and even though I never saw one, my grandma kept me believing that one day I would.

I clearly wasn't thinking when I asked my dad to weigh in on Grandma's stories once, "Dad, have you ever seen a fairy? Grandma knew a lot of them as a kid, but I still haven't seen one."

"Well, I can tell you this: as far as we know, the brain sees what it wants to see. Sometimes people mistake dragonflies for fairies, or planes for UFOs, shadows for ghosts. These are all illusions, and illusions are just brain failures, really. We all experience those."

Typical Mick response. I thought I'd omitted his words from my brain at ten. But when Grandma died, they flooded into my mind like a tsunami of sad facts. I'd always had an imagination like a 3-D printer — I could create anything in the curious walls of my mind. My grandma loved this about me. My dad may be the scientist of the family, but it was Grandma who made me want to be a cosmologist and find out what's going on out there, beyond Earth. I'm even named after her, Alice Jackson, and the juniper fields she always talked about: Juniper Alice Bray is my full name. I seriously used to hate my name. No one I knew had it, and I was already weird enough. Now that it's the only thing connecting me to her, it's my favorite thing about myself. She passed away in her sleep, my parents told me.

"It was peaceful," They promised.

I hoped so.

As just about two more millennia crawled by in that raggedy van, I continued to wallow and play with that lone curl until, for just a moment, and only a moment (nothing more), I was sort-of-kind-of-excited to be in North Carolina. For that fraction of a second, when I saw where I would stay, I was mesmerized.

A pair of brown cows walked past me on the other side of a wooden fence; little pink and brown pigs snorted and squealed in a roomy pen. Chickens scattered every which way, unfenced and free. I felt like I'd made it inside some fantastical storybook home or something. To the left of me was a thriving garden, and beside that stood a brick cottage so viney and rugged you'd think it was made by woodland elves. I must say, reluctantly, I was quite impressed.

As we rolled closer I saw a ball of light pulsing steadily like a heartbeat, slowly growing brighter. *Shit, I'm seeing things again*, I thought.

It took on a shape I couldn't quite make out, and I heard it say, *"Juniper."*

I jumped. Goosebumps bloomed on my flesh.

"Juniper," it repeated.

I closed my eyes. *Breathe, just breathe*, I told myself.

I gawked back to where the light was to find it had disappeared. No one seemed shaken by the voice but me, so I stared straight ahead, like I was a normal person with normal senses and feelings. The van stopped. The soft voice echoed in my mind, like I was in some hollow cave all alone. And I felt alone. I was alone.

I focus on the breathtaking cottage in front of me, as if some sort of reverse psychology could bring my breath back to me. Dad and Ma were getting out but I was still frozen as I saw a sign that read "McKinney Manor." We'd made it.

My initial qualms rushed to me like a wave, and I recalled a major reason I had been apprehensive about the trip, even before Grandma passed. While my dad would be out discovering cures and having the time of his life, I'd be farming. Yes, farming. Last time I'd checked, black families working in fields for free was a little thing I like to call slavery.

I straight up wrote a PowerPoint to my parents titled "Slavery Happened, Let's Not Forget That."

"Nobody in this house is a slave, but let me tell you what you will do this summer — you're gonna work on the McKinney's farm, and that's the end of that." My mom always gets the last word.

And she was right, that really was the end of that. Grandma was in the hospital that day for heart complications, and I went to see her afterwards. She seemed fine, and I remember thinking I couldn't wait till she came back home. She stayed in the guest room at my house, and when she moved in a few years ago, she transformed it into our little sanctuary — beautiful plants everywhere, it always smelled like licorice, and somehow she always had full bowls of candy for me, no matter what. She did end up going home after the hospital, but not long after that, she was gone. I always thought I'd see it coming. In the back of my mind, I just assumed I'd see my grandma off when I turned like 100 years old. But when it happened, it hit me like an avalanche. My grandma thought the PowerPoint idea was clever. She always had my back.

    We stood far from the cottage, but close enough to see a little face peeking out of the bottom half of the front door window, arms and hands pressed on glass. The little hands disappeared, and the door to the two-story cottage creaked open.

    Out came an unassuming, tall black man with muttonchops so classic he looked like an extra out of *Soul Train*, holding a small child with cloud-like dark hair, who had his same kind eyes. Robbie McKinney, or Uncle Robbie to me, since I'd called him that for years.

My Uncle Robbie would then utter two words that were like locks to a door on my summer, "Welcome, welcome!"

    Okay, yes, I know it seems dramatic. "Welcome" is supposed to be, well, welcoming, right? But for me, it was like I'd somehow been able to drift away before, and now I was trapped in this alternate universe wherein I was a farmer, and my grandma wasn't around. It was all officially real. No returning to sender. He leaned in and hugged me, then Mom, in that way people do at funerals. Gentle so as not to break you any more than you've been broken, firm as if trying to hold you together. It made me feel vulnerable and exposed, like I'd just spilled my soul without saying a word.

"Vivian, Juniper! This one's Marci, I don't think you've met," He pointed down at the little girl now hugging my mom's leg.

Mom patted Marci's head and applied a tired grin like a filter, "It's so great to see you again, Rob. It's been too long!"

Her smile was like a lukewarm soup. I remembered meeting Uncle Robbie when I was younger, when he and the McKinneys visited during one of my dad's speaking engagements. He was more bald and grey, but his smile was just as bright and real. He grabbed a bag before gesturing us towards the door, right before I was met with a face that was fresh on my mind: Auntie Elaine. Once dad's study was officially approved, Auntie came up to Hamilton to finalize some things with the university before we'd make our trip. Auntie had gorgeous dark brown skin, strong, thick thighs and shoulder length hair styled with a middle part.

"Now there's my Brother Mick!" Auntie Elaine, with a sunshine smile, embraced my dad like a brother.

"They said it'd never happen!"

She and dad had put the Valeferus project on the back burner for years, so seeing them embrace each other at

Mckinney Manor was like witnessing a team win a championship.

Just as I made it to the door, two more McKinney's patrolled the door like tough guards, arms folded and everything.

"What's good?" The shorter one in the front said.

"Hi." I replied, giving my most neutral stare to this goofy looking dude with arms I'll bet grew before the rest of his body caught up.

This was Robbie, Jr. He's two years younger than me, and has this cocky stroll that's like a failed attempt to look cool. Behind him was a tall girl with a blue-green caesar cut and legs like her mother.

In perfect feline fashion, she flashed the smirk of all smirks, put her hands on her hips, tipped her head to the side and said, "This bout to be a crazy summer."

What does one say to that?

I coughed out my best, "Haha," and kept it moving. Improv isn't my strong suit, and I definitely wasn't trying to embarrass myself around the coolest person there. Okay, yes, we'd literally just met, and you may ask, "How can you even tell she's cool?" Well, when you meet someone cooler than you, cooler than everyone — you just know.

The Mckinney foyer wall was sprinkled with photos that looked nothing like the two kids standing in front of me, much younger, much less cool. I walked further inside and was so focused on not saying something ridiculous that

I tripped over a floor plant by the stairs. And, of course, I had to apologize to an inanimate object,

"Sorry."

I cringe every time I remember that moment.

"Oops! Sorry!" Robbie Jr. chimed in, like the little brother I never wanted.

He couldn't fully hide his southern drawl while mocking my vaguely northern accent, but I didn't critique his tepid jab out loud. It was like my first day of school, and the popular kids were establishing their places on the food chain. I knew where I stood.

"I don't even sound like that." I mumbled to myself, scratching my arm. Luckily the McKinney kids, who I'd assumed could smell fear, didn't know I always itch when I'm nervous.

"How 'bout a tour!" Uncle Robbie corralled a reluctant Junior and Bree.

"That sounds lovely," Mom said. Her expression looked like those awkward photos taken right before a person smiles.

Auntie Elaine put her palm on Uncle Robbie's chest and patted twice before saying, "Honey, I'm sure everybody's tired. Y'all just got here."

Uncle Robbie looked at my mom, and there was an awkward silence. Just enough to feel the painful absence of my grandmother emanating off my mom's cloudy aura. See, me and my mom have a different philosophy. I want everyone to see my void, I want them to see how pissed off

I am. I don't know, it's like me standing strong, holding it down in honor of my grandma. But my mom, well, it's like she didn't want anyone to know how much she missed her mother, like she was fooling anyone. She'd been fake smiling and promising she was "okay" more times than I could count since grandma died. My mother was no actor, but I think some people just didn't care to get the truth out of her so they wouldn't even try. Uncle Robbie, though — he cared.

"You right. Later, I'll give everyone the grand tour." Uncle Robbie breathed. He picked up little Marci, who'd finally unwrapped herself from her mom's leg and said, "Mick, Vivian, how about I show you your room to drop your things off."

Auntie added, "And Bree, you can show Juniper where she'll be staying."

Bree giggled down at me and opened her mouth to speak when —

"Now." Auntie cut her off before she even said a word.

Bree pointed me up the stairs, and I followed, only barely hearing her mumble, "So fucking wack."

She turned her head back to me, eyes squinted and mouth turned up, as if it was my turn to say something edgy. You can probably guess what I did: nothing. I smiled back and kept trekking up the stairs. She rolled her eyes, and I knew I'd failed her test. We got to the second floor, and Bree reached out her hand to open her door, revealing hot pink nails.

I stared up at her and blurted out, "Why'd you shave your head?"

Bree swerved her head around, "What?"

Smooth, June. Real smooth.

I cleared my throat, as if I could clear up how weird I was being and said, "I mean, hi. I'm Juniper. June. I didn't, um, introduce myself so..."

"Ah, okay, June," she nodded and rubbed the green fuzz atop her head, as if trying to spark a fire. "I like how it feels in the wind."

She shrugged and flashed me a toothy grin before strolling over to the second twin bed.

"Nice shirt," She said, as she sat staring at me putting my luggage down.

I'd been called a blerd enough in my life to know that my planet-themed t-shirts were nowhere near fashion-forward, especially to someone as arguably cool as Bree McKinney. I left my roller bag on one of the two plush azure rugs lying between two twin beds covered in black, cloud-themed quilts. I opened my biggest blue suitcase and pulled out a small box that once held my mom's designer watch. In it, I kept a leaf fossil my dad gave me when I was eight. I placed it on the nightstand between us.

"What's that?" Bree asked.

"A fossil."

Immediately after saying it, I knew I was officially the biggest nerd. There was no pretending now.

Where'd you get it?" She asked.

"It's really rare. I dug it up myself on a fossil digging trip..." She walked away from me and I assumed I'd failed at an attempt at the "conversation" thing. I tried again, "So this is your room?"

Nice one, June. I rolled my eyes.

She laughed, "They don't have bedrooms in New York?"

Her smug grin made me nervous.

She nudged me on the shoulder and said, "I'm playin'! It's a joke."

I let out a pathetic giggle.

"You good?"

I smiled but said nothing.

"Okay um. Yeah . . . I'll be downstairs." She galloped out the room. Just like that, she was gone.

As she glided downstairs and swooped past the banister, I decided we couldn't be friends. Sure, she was the only person my age and by far the coolest person at McKinney Manor. Not that I'm that great at making friends with even the friendliest of people, because let's be real, I'm not. That didn't matter to me. All I cared about was that someone I'd never have the guts to talk to in school was someone I'd have to be around, like, a lot. I surveyed the purple room, full of a faint scent of incense, and overcome with a sudden strike of loneliness. If Grandma were there, I wouldn't even have to think about friends. I smiled to myself at what she would've said if I told her about how I felt.

I bet she'd tell me, "That girl ain't studdin' you, so don't you be studdin' her."
She used to say that about the kids at school, and it had become a mantra for me,

"That (insert person of non-interest) ain't studdin' you, so don't you be studdin' (said person)."
I inserted Bree's name and repeated the phrase one more time. I breathed in and let my breath flow out of me as calmly as my body would allow, then I stared out the window because I wasn't quite ready to face people again. The sun outside shone a little brighter through the curtains, and I could have sworn I felt a breeze, even though the windows were closed. I even walked over to check that they were, and sure enough, I was right. I looked back just once more at the oddly bright outdoors before shaking off a blanket of doubt and making my way downstairs.

I heard my dad talking to Uncle Robbie from the kitchen, "Yeah man, it's been a long time coming."

There was a lightness in his voice, like he was smiling. I knew he was talking about the Valeferus.

"Well you know what, brother, it's good to finally have you," Uncle Robbie said.

I remember how angry my dad used to get when the university would deny his annual submission for funding. My dad may be full of himself, but if you work as hard as he does, I guess you can be, right? I'd still feel weird being that openly confident about anything, even if I was amazing at it. Not my dad, though.

"June, is that you?" My dad has this fascinating skill of knowing when I'm around, even if, with every fiber in my being, I feel like he can't see me.

I slumped into the kitchen, where Uncle Robbie stood over the sink, washing greens. My dad was right beside him, arms folded, with his back leaning against the counter.

I hovered in the corner closest to the entryway. There's a lot of stigma about standing in corners, but let me tell you, it's the easiest way to go unnoticed, and you better bet that's where you can find me. Especially since Bree wasn't too far, doing the perfectly fitting task of cutting onions.

I zeroed in on Mom, eyes dim, sitting across from me at the kitchen table. A polite expression, not quite a smile, on her face. I wanted more than anything to hear her say something. *Anything.* I stood there with a nagging feeling at the pit of my stomach. She was thinking of Grandma; she had to be.

Dad took a long, exaggerated inhale and declared how great everything smelled.

Like she'd been revived, Mom got up, reached for an apron on a hook beside the sink, and asked Uncle Robbie what he needed help with.

"No, no! You must be worn out! It's mostly made anyway, you know I'm a pro at these things. Plus, I'm not trying to give away any of these secret recipes just yet."

Mom and Dad laughed. Uncle Robbie was working on a cookbook that summer, one he advertised as "health conscious with some Jamaican flavor." He grabbed a heavy bowl out of the fridge.

A wrinkle on Mom's forehead formed, as her mouth curled up and finally she muttered, "Well, all right, I guess I could use a power nap," and exited the room like a wind-up toy on its last few winds.

I left my corner and backed out a little bit more towards the stairs. I wasn't sure where I'd go, but definitely didn't plan to stick around.

"Can I or June help with anything?"

My dad just had to ruin it.

"Don't you wanna see how we run things over here in the South?" Bree dragged out "South" like she was making fun of her own accent.

"Uh…" I stammered.

What do you do when you know what you *should* say doesn't fit what you want to say? Bree made her way over and folded her arms.

"What? You don't wanna cut onions! I'm shocked." She playfully nudged my shoulder. *What is with this girl and shoulder nudges?*

I knew if I stayed, Uncle Robbie would clearly want to have conversations. You know, those things I like to avoid.

I was still deep in thought when Uncle Robbie said, "If you're not too tired."

That was my out. You might say I could have left right at that moment and seeked solace in Bree's room. I was tired and sad and my introversion was all too present in my mind. I could have said, *Yes, Uncle Robbie, I'm wiped out.* But I didn't.

"Okay," is what I said instead.

Yes, you have every right to roll your eyes at me. I did, too. I didn't want to hurt Uncle's feelings even though I probably wouldn't have. I wanted to be more okay than I was. I was taking a page out of my mom's book.

"You know what would make this a party? Some wine." Bree wriggled her eyebrows at her dad.

Uncle Robbie pointed a spatula at us and said, "Bree, hush. Juniper, how 'bout you set the table, if ya could? Dishes and everything are over here."

He pointed to a cabinet with a window beside the sink.

"Okay," I mumbled.

Bree giggled, and I started to itch. Uncle Robbie began asking me questions, because of course he would.

"So what would Ms. June be doing right now, if not all the way down here in the Carolinas?"

I thought hard. I thought around and around in circles, trying to avoid the space in my mind where Grandma lived. If I wasn't in North Carolina, if I was doing exactly what I wanted to do, I would have been working on a crossword puzzle with my grandma in my living room. On a Sunday. When Grandma was alive, Sundays were always reserved for brain games after church. She had a lot of vintage *New York Times* newspapers she'd just pull out, and we'd decode.

I used to be really bad at them, but she'd always tell me, "Girl, ain't nobody good till they practice."

And I ran with that phrase, until one day, my time beat hers by exactly two minutes. I never let her forget it, since it was the only time I won. I reminded myself of her advice the year I started swimming. I was eight, and my parents moved to a house that was only a few blocks from a community center. I started taking lessons and immediately fell in love, even though I wasn't very good. But I kept thinking: *Ain't nobody good till they practice.* Now I'm actually pretty good, if I do say so myself.

"June you alright over there?" Uncle Robbie had put his big spoon down and looked visibly concerned.

I must have zoned out.

"Oh! Yeah, uh . . . No I'm fine. I, uh, was thinking I'd probably be reading, I guess? I read a lot," I lied.

"Oh, that's a good hobby to have. You hear that, Bree?"

Bree's face lit up, and she exclaimed, "You ever read Jacqueline Woodson? Her stuff is so queer, oh my God. Like gay, for real, for real."

Blood rushed to my cheeks. I've never been happier to be dark-skinned.

"Um . . . no." I was shocked. I couldn't believe she said that out loud.

I'd never actually uttered the word "queer" around my parents, and even now, I don't think I could. The breezy way she spoke, though, I could tell she had. Plus, Uncle Robbie didn't even flinch. My parents weren't, like, homophobic or anything. We just didn't talk about queerness, dating, or sex or anything like that. My mom's idea of "the talk" was giving me a very scientific explanation about hetero sex and then handing me a pamphlet about abstinence, "the safest option", with a tiny blurb about other contraception in the back. I knew then the McKinneys were nothing like my family, but I hadn't decided yet if I was okay with that.

Uncle Robbie set out a Jamaican fish dish, greens with dried tomato, a pot of soup, a bed of rice and beans. The table was dressed with flowers Aunt Elaine had brought in from the garden, and the smell of herbal tea complimented the house.

"Everything smells wonderful." Mom yawned and leaned on the kitchen door. She looked like she'd closed her eyes for a time, but got no sleep.

Uncle Robbie gently herded us to our seats, "Go'on then, sit!"

I sat on the corner closest to Mom by the entry way, totally prepared to bounce at the first sign of discomfort. Not that I'd actually leave, I wasn't that bold, but the fact that I could was comforting enough. Robbie Jr. brought in two other chairs from the living room, making the already small space seem a bit claustrophobic. The scent of tangy spices filled the room, while the evening sun cast warm hues around the table. Even with the extra clutter and heat, the little McKinney kitchen still kept a certain level of charm.

"Soup, soup!" Little Marci shouted. Clearly this was one of the few food terms she'd mastered.

Aunt Elaine appeared again with Marci on her hip, my Dad right behind them. Dad washed his hands at the sink.

Uncle Robbie was the last to join us at the table. He kept searching the pantry as if there was more to do, even though every dish he said he'd make was already out. He sat between Mom and Auntie and surveyed the table one last time. I admired the pleased look on his face as he said, "Eat up!"

Mom went straight for the rice, Robbie Jr. only played with some of the fish dish, and Bree piled on a little bit of everything. She didn't seem to care when her food began to run together. It grossed me out. Everyone was smacking on something or other by this time, except me. I just watched and thought of what my grandma might have had. She would have loved the fish. I'll bet she would have insisted on making something. I thought my grandma would be telling a story about her garden now, and everyone would be sitting in awe as she animated every little detail with her hands.

I'd zoned out again. I stared at nothing straight ahead, and she appeared. I was thinking about her, and she just materialized in front of me. I froze. I wanted to gasp, but my mouth stayed fixed. She was surrounded by her garden in the middle of the kitchen, and I sat there dumbfounded, like, *How was no one else seeing this?* It was as real as the rice and beans on my father's plate.

Her expression was serene as she floated there, weightless, smack-dab in the middle of the McKinneys' kitchen. I told my brain I needed to pinch myself, but my body refused.

"Juniper. Soon. Soon you'll see," she said.

"How? When?" I wanted to ask.

I wanted to scream. I knew I'd look crazy.

"Juniper. June!" Bree slapped me on the shoulder.

Just like that I was back to reality, or whatever life without my grandma is supposed to be called.

"My dad's been talking to you for like three hours," Bree cracked up.

I realized I was still shaking.

"Are you okay?" My mom asked me.

I nodded.

"I was asking, what's your favorite subject in school? Mick says you love science just like him, huh? I was a pretty big history buff myself."

Still frazzled, I nodded, "He's right."

I couldn't focus. All I could think about was what I'd just seen. *Did I even see it?*

I was tempted to ask Bree if she'd noticed anything, but she couldn't have. She was chomping on whatever was in her mouth with the calmest obliviousness. I felt off and weird and unstable, just like I had in the car ride here, with the voices and the odd imagery. Still, I shook it off. I didn't know any better, and quite frankly, I was too scared to delve into the truth. Looking back, clearly this was a moment to reflect, but just stay with me as I do some of the world's best ignoring.

Uncle Robbie had already moved on.

My dad was now asking Bree things. "Are you still drawing?"

Bree nodded her head "yes" with her mouth full.

Aunt Elaine added, "Bree draws on reasonable surfaces these days, a tad different than her past work."

Aunt and Uncle cracked up at this. Bree grumbled a bit, stuffed her face further. It's like as long as she had food on her plate, she was content, regardless of the circumstance.

She cleared out one half of her mouth and said, "Some of the best artists do street art."

"Yeah, yeah, don't speak with your mouth full," Aunt Elaine laughed.

Auntie told a story of how Bree's "work" had shown up in the news once. Bree and her friends used to recreate scenes from various kids' cartoons and replaced the faces with teachers they didn't like. It took two months for the police to figure out it was Bree, and they only caught her because one of Bree's friends' parents happened to be driving down a usually quiet street in the city while they were drawing.

As Auntie spoke, Bree looked like she was torn between a dramatic exit and going for seconds. She chose the latter. Bree ate, nonchalant, while our parents cracked up for what had to be an eternity.

When they finally quieted down, Bree said, "Oh my god, that was too funny!"

Her words were soaked in sarcasm. Aunt Elaine shot Bree a look I knew very well. I returned to my thoughts, while Robbie Jr. played a game involving picking up and dropping the food on his plate.

Meanwhile, I grew more and more anxious as no mention of my grandmother had come up. I wondered how my parents had managed to leave out someone who'd played such a prominent role in our travel plans and our reason for being there. I imagined I was bold enough to call her out on the erasure.

"Mom, remember the time Grandma made a whole feast out of a bunch of leftover rice a few greens and some turkey bacon in our fridge?" I'd say.

"Remember how Grandma was going to sit right next to me, right now?" I'd shout.

But I didn't. I just sat there. Brewing.

Bree leaned into me and cooed, "I bet you're excited about work in the morning, huh?"

I hesitated, "What am I doing . . . exactly?"

"Well, we usually start out with feeding the pigs and go on from there. It'll seem like a lot, but you'll get used to it," Aunt Elaine started.

"Lol, 'we,'" Bree whispered loudly in my ear.

Aunt Elaine gave Bree another one of those death stares. Lips pursed, eyes focused and fierce. I had a feeling Bree got that look a lot.

I couldn't understand how easily words just fell out of Bree's mouth. It took me a lot to say "hi," let alone anything else. Another thing I knew I wouldn't say out loud is I secretly admired Bree for being bold enough to say whatever she wanted. But since she had no boundaries, I also didn't trust her. I tuned in to the table again, like plugs had been taken out of my ears. Bowls of rice and beans were down to their last few spoonfuls, except for my own. I had only a few bites and not much of an appetite. Dishes hit the sink, and Auntie Elaine was clearing the table. I grabbed my plate and put it with the pile.

Bree grasped me by the arm as she pulled me all the way up to her room and slammed the door behind us, "Friends don't let friends do dishes."

We'd made it to the twin beds, but I was still stuck on the awkward part where she called me her "friend." *Friends? Really?* I barely knew her, so this whole "friend" concept felt way too premature for us.

I mean, I know you're probably thinking I, of all people, shouldn't be so picky. I kind of didn't . . . have any friends. But I wasn't just going to let some sarcastic, albeit interesting, girl I barely know take that title. Friendship meant more to me than it did to a lot of people. I mean, my grandma was my best friend. Not many people could live up to that, and I didn't think Bree had it in her. She fished around in the drawer beside her bed and pulled out a lighter. She lifted her mattress strategically and took out a small crumpled box.

I took a seat on my new, incredibly soft bed and played my own version of chill. I sunk into what felt like memory foam and folded my arms. *Be cool. Just be cool, it's not that hard,* I tried convincing myself.

Bree opened the window just slightly, pulled out a cigarette from the little silver box, and lit it, taking a deep drag. I scratched my cheek and then my neck. I was covered in invisible hives, which frankly was cramping my attempt at being chill. So, of course, at the most inopportune time, she turned to me with the cigarette, only to catch me scratching the hell out of my shoulder.

"The fuck is wrong with you?" She laughed.

I tried changing the subject, "Man, I still have tons to unpack."

I unzipped my suitcase with no real intention of unpacking, but the act of doing something else calmed me a bit. I felt Bree near me and turned around to find her pointing a cigarette at my face.

"You cool?" Bree raised an eyebrow.

I glanced at her quickly and moved to "unpack" more clothes.

"Er, yeah, I'm cool," I said, still unpacking. Still avoiding.

Crisis averted, I thought, not actually knowing that her question translated to: "Do you smoke?" I think she knew I had no idea, because she just kept smoking, not even responding to my awkwardness.

"We're gonna have so much fun tomorrow."

"Yeah, I guess," I mumbled.

The smoke started to feel overwhelming when I began to realize this wasn't just a cigarette…

"Hahaha, I was being sarcastic. We're definitely not 'bout to have fun tomorrow."

She took another drag, the smoke lingering in my nostrils and causing my throat to get scratchy.

"Oh," I tried to make my cough sound like a laugh. I failed.

She put out her joint and placed it neatly back in her box, before putting it back under her bed. Then she grabbed a pillow and threw it at my head.

"Geez," I said reflexively.

"Loosen up!" Bree hopped on her bed and allowed herself to fall into crossed legs.

How do you have so much energy? I thought.

I looked away. I felt old. I felt like the oldest fifteen-year-old that ever lived. I mean, maybe I wasn't cut out to spend quality time with people my age. Maybe I was meant to find another 83-year-old person to bond with.

She leaned back on her bed, belly up and arms behind her head, "I had a feeling you'd be super, duper low-key."

"Low-key?" I asked.

"Yeah, like mad quiet, mad introverted. Don't get hype, usually." She stared up at the ceiling as she spoke.

"Oh." I responded.

For some reason I translated "low-key" to boring in my mind. I figured she was totally disappointed with how little I spoke, how awkward I was. I turned away; I didn't want her to see I was hurt by what she said, even though I told myself it didn't bother me. I didn't even want to be her friend, so why would I care? My throat tightened.

Well, at least I'm not the perfect cliché of a rebellious teen.

"I'm not . . . low key," I finally muttered, even though I know I probably am.

"Yeah, okay," she said between chuckles, as she settled in on her bed. She started pulling off her socks and said,

"I'm going to sleep. It's about to be a long day tomorrow."

I was flabbiness personified. I slumped to the bathroom. That night, I dreamed about all I could have said, but I'd wake up forgetting it all.

Chapter Two

I woke up to Bree hovering over my bed with a toothbrush hanging from her mouth.

"Hey," she said, toothpaste foaming over her teeth.

I sat up, blinking several times to see past the morning brain fog, "What?"

"You're not wearin' shorts are you?" she pointed to my neatly placed jean shorts on the drawer in front of us.

"Why?" I asked flatly.

Good, good. Try to sound disinterested, I thought.

"I mean, you *can*. If you want to get shit all over your ankles, then by all means, wear shorts." Through the foam, she flashed me a mischievous smile and trotted to the bathroom.

Embarrassed by my outfit, I stuffed it in the drawer and pulled out my one pair of jeans, which I'd worn a hole in at the knees, kept on the ratty gray shirt I'd slept in, and threw on my old space camp hoodie. Bree came back in, teeth brushed, wearing black overalls, a long-sleeved top, and heavy work boots. She laughed as I groggily laced up my shoes.

"Welp, I'll be in the back, preppin' the pig's slop!" she announced before galloping down the stairs.

I hadn't even fully rubbed the sleep out of my eyes. I checked my watch: 5:30 a.m. In spite of loving mornings, this was early for me. I usually woke up around 8 a.m. without any alarms.

I took my time getting downstairs in hopes she'd be done with the pigs before I came down. I had a feeling I'd be outside for a while.

It had to have been fifteen minutes since Bree left me, but as I walked out, she was just standing there next to a huge wheelbarrow full of unidentifiable mush. She checked her bare wrist and shook her head. The sarcasm with this girl.

I curled my lip in annoyance, too tired for a rebuttal.

The mud under my sneakers oozed around my feet. The pigs behind us squealed like they knew what was up. I imagined I was in my grandma's quiet garden. A cool breeze wrapped around my skin.

"Hahaha, what are you doing? Here." Bree pulled out a pair of latex gloves and handed them to me.

When I had them on straight, she handed me a bucket of water and gestured for me to tag along. She pushed the wheelbarrow, opened the pigpen just slightly, and tipped the wheelbarrow, letting pig food cover the front of the pen. I stood there in either disgust or awe, as four brown pigs attacked the mush like it was the first meal they'd eaten in years. A smaller one paced back and forth behind the others, too little to push through the big guys.

Bree reached into her pocket and pulled out a pastry, "Hey! Here ya go, Wilbur!"

Wilbur. Like in Charlotte's Web. I secretly gushed at the reference to one of my favorite childhood books. The little piglet waddled over and ate the pastry in one bite. It was comfortable with Bree, I could tell.

"Now the chickens," Bree barked, as she marched off.

But I couldn't stop staring at the little pig. Its little eyes were so lively and soft. I know it's strange, but I had this nagging feeling it was about to speak. But I trailed off. I knew I was just being weird. I knew I had been strange since the trip started, and told myself to stop being so fantastical. Mick Bray would not approve.

I was more than ready when we finally went inside. I caught a glimpse of the clock when we went inside: 7:15 a.m. I was starting to think the earliness of our chores was just an added torture. Bree led me back out, and I assumed we were almost done, maybe just putting some things away. I don't know why I'd make that assumption. I'm more optimistic than I think I am. Because instead, Bree grabbed a gardener's tool belt off the shed near the chickens and looped it around her waist.

"What else could there be?" I thought I'd only said it in my mind.

"Girl, we ain't half done," She laughed.

We were both sweating, though it wasn't even that hot outside.

"What?" I ripped off my gloves.

Between chuckles she said, "You might wanna keep the gloves on. We've got a whole garden to work on."

The garden. Uncle Robbie and Auntie Elaine were avid herbalists and gardeners. Auntie Elaine did most of the herb work for her studies, and Uncle Robbie grew vegetables for his cooking. It was a whole elaborate setup. If this were happening a few months ago, I'd be ecstatic. I'd probably have volunteered before the McKinneys even asked me. But that day, the thought of working on a garden made me sad and lonely in a way I couldn't shake. But then at the same time, gardening was my solace. Back home, I took over Grandma's garden after her arthritis made it difficult for her to manage it. Mom even told me she thought I'd inherited Grandma's green thumb. I took pride in gardening in a way I thought Bree would laugh at. So I didn't say anything.

I just put my gloves back on and said, "Cool."

In the very back of the garden, there was a patch of dark manure in several lumpy piles. Beside all the fresh blooms, herbs, and vegetables, there was a rotten mess of old, half-eaten veggies atop the manure. That's where Bree was headed. She snagged two gardening spades from her work belt and handed one to me.

"You think you're sweating now! This shit' bout to be a waterfall." She crouched down on her knees and began to dig.

"So basically, these shit piles are about to be plants, thanks to us." She fished in her belt pocket and pulled out seeds.

"What's that?" I asked.

"Strawberries," she said, wiggling her eyebrows and speaking like a cheesy talk show host. I'm not gonna lie, that made me smile.

I wiped sweat from my brow. As hot as it was, I could still see why Grandma loved gardening so much. It's hard not get lost in the beauty of nature when you're surrounded by it. I took off my gloves and felt the dirt between my fingers. I dug into the dirt and started planting. I was comfortable for the first time since I'd gotten to North Carolina.

We'd been working in relative silence for a while, when suddenly Bree sat back in the dirt. I felt her eyes on me. I panicked at the likelihood this silence wouldn't last.

"So, I hear you had a farm back in your place," she mused.

I was right. I shrugged, attempting to mask my drum of a heartbeat, "It was actually my grandma's farm. Not mine."

I paused. I could have said more, but I really didn't feel like it.

The silence dragged making me uncomfortable, so I kept talking, "I only visited a few times before they sold it."

I really did plan on shutting up after that. I really did.

But I kept speaking, "Actually, my grandma used to play in a garden like this when she was little."

Why couldn't I stop talking?

"She used to tell me about how she'd play with little creatures, she called them fairies. It was really cool. I dunno, they were—"

"—Wait! Stop. Rewind. She played with fairies? Like, fairy fairies? Was she all there?" She chortled briefly before covering her mouth, like she'd retroactively realized how offensive she was being.

"Yes," I dropped the seed into the dirt.

"I'm sorry, I forgot she . . . died. I swear I wasn't even thinking about it." Bree said.

But she'd already said enough. I stood up.

She rose with me, "June, I was playin'. I mean, are we really trying to say that's not weird, though? I'm not judging you. It was just funny, I don't know—"

"Seriously, you're such an asshole!" I blurted.

The words felt so strange but I meant them. I was shrinking by the second. I knew my parents wanted us to get along, but all I could think about was how alone I felt while she laughed at me. I wanted nothing more than to talk to my grandma back in my own bedroom back home. Bree's obliviousness made it worse. She had no idea how amazing Grandma was.

"I said I was sorry!" she exclaimed.

"Did you ever stop to think that maybe the stuff you say isn't funny?" I asked with no desire for a response.

I got closer to the door by the second.

"What else am I supposed to say?" she shouted after me.

"Ugh!"

The memory of the first time my Grandma told me her fairy story flashed into my head. My grandpa was still alive and he and Grandma still lived on her childhood farm. I couldn't have been more than five. I was sitting at the living room table in Grandpa's lap, Grandma across from me. We were all eating some of her infamous carrot cake with some tea and she'd just cut me a slice too big for me to finish. She always gave me more sweets than I needed, but the exact amount I wanted. Grandpa loved her stories just as much as I did and he believed them too. I remember him giving affirming "Mmhmms" whenever Grandma would tell me it's okay for me to believe.

I'd made it to the door and my memory faded. My reality sunk in and I began brewing again. I marched into the house and slammed the front door behind me. I planned on locking myself in her room and never leaving, but that idea was trampled by someone I was also hoping to avoid: my mom.

"June, that you? You done with the chores already?" she asked me from the kitchen.

I locked my lips. I didn't feel like speaking. I just wanted to sleep like Rip Van Winkle and let three months pass until I woke up in Hamilton again.

"Yes," I said finally, staring at the ground.

She spoke in a warm but stern tone, "Hey. Sit down."

Mom sipped tea from a mug that had cat ears, which I'd usually find amusing, and asked, "Rough day on the farm?"

I shrugged, "I hate it here."

The words poured out of me.

"Give it time. It hasn't even been two days," she took another sip.

"Two days is long enough," I muttered under my breath.

She carefully put down her mug and glared at me, as if searching for the truth. She waited for me to look directly into her eyes before saying,

"Okay, look. I know..." She began, her hand on her temple.

Her eyes were misty, her mouth turned down, but she looked way too tired to cry.

"We both miss her. It's hard, it really is. But I need you to give this place a chance. You know she'd want you to enjoy yourself, make friends, learn new things..."

She rubbed her temples. I thought of Bree. If she was the only "friend" I was supposed to make, then my odds weren't looking so good. We sat there for a moment. I didn't respond. I just stared at the mug until it didn't look like a mug anymore.

"Are you finished with your work?" she asked me.

I nodded. I heard Bree slam the door so hard it caused the spoon beside my mom's mug to rattle. She lunged up the stairs, and Mom glanced back at me again. She looked like she wanted to say something, but didn't. Just as I was deciding how to get away, my dad lumbered in. I really just wanted some solitude.

"Viva, I'm going to go into the city..." My dad trailed off when he saw us. He visibly gauged the tension in the room, before he patted her shoulder and said, "Hey."

His voice slowed, lowered, and he repeated himself, "Do you need anything? I'll be in the city for a bit."

Mom shook her head, and they shared a moment that, as the only kid living at home, I knew all too well: the "what happened this time" look.

"Can I go?" I asked, very prepared to avoid whatever they might try to talk to me about.

Mom nodded, and I made a quick exit, stopping at the top of the stairs. They were going to talk about me. I knew it.

It was quiet for a moment, and then I heard Mom say, "I really need her to give this place a chance."

It grew quiet again, and I thought my mom might be crying.

Finally, Dad chimed in, "You know what? How about I take June with me everyday?"

Silence.

"Think about it—she used to love helping me with small projects when she was younger. I think this would be really good for her."

He was right, I loved helping him with his projects, and I really missed helping, too.

"That might be good," Mom said after a while.

Yes! I thought.

She continued, "But what about Bree, and the farm?"

No, no, no, no.

"Well, Bree could go, too! She needs to spend time with people her own age. And Junior can hold down the fort for a few weeks, he knows the farm. Elaine was just talking about how much he's loving this time off, but he's not doing anything else."

In seconds, my dad turned a great idea into a nightmare. Bree and me didn't mix. We were oil and water, vinegar and milk. A toxic pair. If he'd seen us in the garden, he'd know.

"Ok. Let's run it by Elaine and Rob, see what they think," Mom responded.

Dad said, "Ok, I'll see you when I get back, then."

I waited for the sound of the front door closing before I snuck down the stairs and quietly tiptoed outside. I needed to be alone.

I stopped at the pigsty to talk to Wilbur. Something about him made me feel at ease. He stared up at me with those peaceful eyes and made soft snuffling sounds, like he recognized me.

"Hi, little Wilbur."

I could have sworn he nodded at me.

"Do *you* even like Bree? I'll bet you don't," I said, as I rubbed his fuzzy back.

"You're the cutest thing, you know that?" I stroked Wilbur's head. He snuggled in closer to me and I felt a kind breeze surround me and I felt calmer than I had in some time.

Suddenly, Wilbur looked at me and said, "Welcome, Juniper."

I jumped back, gawking at the little creature. I had the urge to run, but my feet were fixed to the ground.

"I'm . . . sorry?" I spluttered.

I looked around. Maybe someone else was speaking, and I was just seeing things. He looked so unassuming, snorting like he hadn't just spoken.

And then he said, "It's okay."

I gasped and covered my mouth.

"Don't be afraid. I'm on your side." His voice was as grunty as his fur was fuzzy.

"Oh my god, oh my god, oh my god."

I backed away, but didn't leave. Apparently I was more curious than I was afraid.

"What is happening right now?" I thought out loud.

"You'll find out soon enough." He began to walk away.

He looked back and said, "Good day, Juniper," And trotted off.

"Wait!" I shouted after him.

He kept walking all the way to the other side of the pig pen. I stood in front of the sty, dumbfounded.

What the actual fuck?

I needed answers. I paced around the garden, past bright yellow and crimson flowers lining the fence. A dirt pathway circled around a quaint potato patch, leading up to an old stone fountain. Atop the fountain was a carved stone angel, with an ambiguous expression that reminded me of the Mona Lisa. I'd seen sculptures like it before, but there was something special about this one. I was studying its face closely when something bright in the palm of its hand caught my eye.

At first it was a still, small light, like a hovering bulb reflecting silver flecks. It flickered and waved, as if trying to communicate with me. It floated away from the angel's hand and toward the tomatoes, and without a second thought, I followed. I tailed that ball of light all the way through the garden, until it burned so bright I had to turn away.

When I looked again, the light had darkened to red, then to black, and created a void in space, right there, right in front of me. The void grew until in front of me all I saw was darkness. I reached for the darkness even though I should resist. My cares fell away, all I wanted in that moment was to see what was on the other side. I stepped forward once, then again a little bit closer, but I moved too slowly. The portal closed, and the light was gone as if it were never there.

I raced around the fountain, but I couldn't find any remnants of the beam of light that started it all. I could hear my dad's voice in my head saying, "Illusions are just brain failures," and I repeated it over and over like a mantra. I told myself I was just seeing things. It was only an illusion. It *had* to be an illusion. Every weird thing I'd seen lately had to be my brain playing tricks on me.

I pretended to read a book I'd found on the living room shelf. Bree was still in her room, and I was too shaken up to stay outside. I needed to see someone other than Bree to feel normal again. I felt like I was losing my mind.

Finally, I heard my dad and Auntie Elaine arrive. Auntie leaned on the opening of the living room and asked, "You made it. How'd it go?"

"It was okay," I lied.

"Just okay? Well, that's no good!" My dad exclaimed, and Auntie clearly thought this was hilarious.

My dad gave me a big smooch on the cheek. He had a way of making me feel like he couldn't wait to see me. He'd look me directly in the eyes, like I was the sole reason for his smile. I was warm and, for just a moment, almost forgot all that had happened less than an hour ago.

"Let's get back to the lab in a bit? After food," Auntie asked my dad.

She started to leave.

"Right, all right. Oh, but wait!" Dad called back to her.

"Oh, that's right: we've got some fun news for you girls," Auntie quipped.

"I think it'll cheer you up," Dad said.

He looked so sincere standing there, clearly having no idea I already knew what he'd say.

"Wait a sec, Mick. I want them to find out together," Auntie cooed.

I braced myself as Auntie called Bree down.

Dad waited for a reluctant Bree to sit on the opposite side of the living room before shouting, "Ok. Here's the big news. You won't be doing farm work anymore! We all agreed you and Bree can come help us on site. What do you think of that?"

Bree peered at my dad. The awkward silence was becoming unbearable, so I said, "That's really cool, Dad."

I did my best to look excited, but all I could think about was everything I'd witnessed since getting here.

"It'll be like old times," Dad grinned, as he patted my shoulder.

I carried on my fake smile. I didn't want to hurt his feelings.

"What if we'd rather do farm work, though?" Bree's arms were folded, her eyes red like she'd been crying. Or smoking.

"Bree. This is what's happening now. You have a problem with that?" Auntie mirrored Bree's arm fold, which then made Bree drop her arms like some Jedi mind trick.

"No," Bree said finally, deflated.

My dad jumped right back in, as oblivious as ever, "So! No need to get up at the break of dawn tomorrow, all right? I'll come wake you up to start packing the car around 9 or 10."

I nodded, and he patted us both on the shoulder as he left. Bree rolled her eyes and walked out behind him.

I sat there alone and watched my life quietly turning upside-down as I sat in the living room.

CHAPTER THREE

Even though we didn't have to get up as early, I took it upon myself to get up anyway to go to the garden. I couldn't get Wilbur and that strange vortex out of my mind. I snuck out while it was still dark and hung out there until sunrise. I ignorantly floated around that farm while a lot of nothing happened. No ball of light, no talking Wilbur. Just me, the sun, and the morning breeze. Every step closer to the door, I itched more at the thought that I'd have to spend the rest of my day with Bree.

Later, Dad told me that he, Mom, and the McKinneys had pitched in to pay their neighbor's teen son to help Junior out around the farm. Bree and I would work with our parents four days a week and the farm for one and Robbie would do the rest, and see how that felt. My main issue with this set up? There was no Bree-free option.

Auntie Elaine had an old, blue Ford cargo van with the last row of seats gutted out. The McKinneys kept the van behind the house in a makeshift garage that looked like it had been thrown together in six seconds. For the van, Auntie squeezed between the wall and van door to back it out.

Before we even left the house, Auntie had already assigned us our first task. We were supposed to pack the lab equipment in the back in a "neat and organized manner." So, of course, Bree plopped the first bag in like it was made of bricks. I sneered. A lot of Dad's equipment was made of glass (see: super fragile). I jerked the next bag out of Bree's careless hands, intending to place it neatly next to the first, but she pushed my arm, making the bag fumble to the ground instead of safely in the trunk. My blood boiled.

"All right, all right, enough of that. June, you know not to play around with the equipment," said Dad.

"I wasn't—"

My fist was so tight it might explode. Not only was she careless, she made me look that way too. I was furious, but I couldn't get words to come out of my mouth. I was just standing there gritting my teeth with eyes watering like a hot pot ready to bubble over. And so I exhaled and focused all that energy on packing the rest of the equipment. I neatly shoved Bree to the side when she tried to help me.

She threw up her hands, said, "Less work for me!" and started playing on her phone.

Good riddance, I thought.

After I'd packed every last box as strategically as I possibly could, Bree and I got in and sat on either end of the back seat, looking out opposing windows and pretending the other didn't exist. Between us sat the portable microscope, snug as a newborn baby. It was a nice excuse to keep our distance, though I knew we'd have been just as far away if it weren't there.

Uncle Robbie sent us off with bags of individually wrapped homemade granola, oranges, and water. I wasn't hungry, but Dad warned us we would be later. The site was about an hour out, after all.

I gazed out the window and imagined I was alone, which was a much more difficult task than I'd hoped, with Bree tapping to some silent beat with her leg on the door. I wanted to be home so bad I wished for it. I literally mouthed the word "home," like I was Dorothy from the *Wizard of Oz.* Not that I really thought something would happen, but come on, I was desperate. Nothing about the endless fields, clear springs, and forest-green valleys reminded me of my usual grungy, industrial New York town. I never thought I'd think it, but I missed the torn-up roads of Hamilton.

I could tell we were almost there by the plant life spilling out around us. It was the sort of beauty that's so objective it doesn't matter what mood you're in—you'll notice. We parked beside yellow corn lily blossoms. Auntie slowed as a family of red deer galloped right past the van. I loved that my dad would be researching in a spot like that.

I geeked out in spite of myself and said, "Dad, this is so cool," before totally wishing I could retract my statement.

Bree's exasperated breath said everything I didn't want to hear. I composed myself, tried to look a little less eager.

"Welcome to our new office!" Dad, delighted, hopped out of the van and headed for the trunk.

His liveliness was contagious, and I felt proud to be an accomplice. The forest looked alive, and beckoned me with its enchantment. I almost didn't notice Bree roll her eyes.

I ignored her and grabbed hold of a packed tent by the handle. Putting it together would be our first job on site. I'd built tents a few times before. Once on a daddy-daughter camping trip when I was nine, and another time during summer camp when I was eleven. I loved it both times, and the steps came pretty easy to me.

Regardless, I didn't want to seem like a know-it-all with Bree. I know, I shouldn't have cared after all that went down, but I did.

And so when she folded her arms and scowled, "I don't know how to set up a freakin' tent," I responded with, "Yeah . . . me neither."

In spite of the fact that she already knew I was a nerd, in spite of the fact that we'd already established she's the worst, I still wanted cool points from her.

But then Dad walked over and ruined everything, as dads do, "What are you talking about? You've pitched tents plenty of times!"

"Word?" She let out a hearty laugh that I definitely don't think this situation warranted, and I shrunk to about one inch tall.

Since I'd failed to fool anyone, I decided to keep my mouth shut and get to work. I spotted an area with the least plants. I unbagged the tent and started pitching it on my own. She was unreadable, either secretly watching my every move or totally zoning out. I felt her gaze on my back as I staked each corner to the ground. As I finished, Bree began slow clapping behind me.

Slowly, she began to pick up speed and smiled, "Good job. Bravo!"

I brushed off my dusty knees and edged right past her, scowling as best I knew how.

We'd pitched the tent, set up the workstation, and prepped the equipment. Well, I should say I did those things. Bree spent the majority of her time snacking and half-heartedly labeling Dad's notes in a file folder he brought along. When I wasn't thinking about Bree, I was actually having fun. Each time I focused, I'd forget, for just a moment, that she

Jaz Joyner

was there. My little pockets of bliss. I finished all the tasks on my list much sooner than I'd hoped and was excited for more. I wanted more pockets of bliss, more moments that I actually enjoyed on this trip.

"Dad!" I called out, even though he was only a few feet away.

He was so engrossed in his project, I had to call him several times. I peered into the forest and anticipated a mini adventure. I imagined what would happen if I just left right then, into the forest, away from everyone. I shook my head. *Juniper Bray doesn't do adventures*, I reminded myself. By the time he looked up, I could have un-pitched and re-pitched the entire tent.

"Dad, I'm done with everything!"

"Good! That was quick," he chirped. "What do you think, E, should we give them a break?"

"I don't know . . . looks like we could use some help labeling a few hundred of these files..." Then she laughed, "Yeah, sure. Go ahead."

"Thank you!" I cheered.

"Finally," Bree plopped down on a rock, where I assumed she'd stay for the rest of our free time.

I, on the other hand, couldn't wait to find out what was beyond the site. I planned to follow the sound of a stream beyond the trees I'd been hearing since we arrived.

"Have fun," Dad said. "Stay close. I'll let you know if we need you."

60

I had gotten hungry and decided I needed to eat before I took off to explore. Luckily, Bree had dropped the snack bags beside a tree, so I went over and grabbed one, chomped down my first handful of granola, and headed down a faded path. I had no intention of inviting her. I'd been spellbound by the forest since we got there, and it's not like I needed an excuse to leave Bree in the dust.

I was doing it: I was exploring. If it weren't for the muddy pathway, I'd have thought I was the first in hundreds of years to set foot there. The forest was so green, like nothing I'd ever seen. I gawked, mesmerized, as a rabbit bounced from one tree trunk to the next and scurried away.

"So cute," I mused out loud.

"Talkin' to yourself?"

I jumped at the sound of Bree's voice. She mosied over to me and planted her hands on her hips.

"God! What are you doing?" Her sheer presence annoyed me.

"Frolicking in the woods, like you."

Ugh. Was she ever not *the worst?*

I folded my arms and asked, "Did you follow me?"

"Don't flatter yourself," she rolled her eyes. "I'm just going to the water over there."

My whole mood was deflated. She had to be talking about the same water I was going to, but I kept walking with every intention of losing her. I moved quickly over plush moss and shimmering placid puddles, while Bree tread right beside me. The trickling water got closer and closer, until a modest waterfall came into view. It flowed into a small pool surrounded by moss-covered rocks. I moved in for a view of the water clear enough to see glittering pink fish swimming just below the surface. I was still considering jumping in when Bree started to kick off her shoes. She threw her clothes into a pile on a stump near the water. In just her underwear, she jumped in, wading at first, her legs disappearing a little bit more every moment until she was hip-deep in the water.

"It's warm," she said.

I gawked as Bree moved farther toward the waterfall. I was still pissed I wasn't there on my own, but also intrigued by her. I hated how naturally bold she was, or maybe I envied it. I couldn't tell which. At first I was too much of a wimp to join her. But then something drew me in despite myself. I stepped in, only thinking enough to throw off my shoes before I glided towards the waterfall.

I waded through as quickly my heavy jeans would allow. I made it to the curtain where Bree was already running her hands through the cascade.

"Well, look at you!" Bree quipped.

My curls started to frizz from the fine mist all around us.

"I'll bet you won't go under," She stretched her hand stretched toward the fall.

"Maybe I will," I said, feeling bold.

Suddenly, her hand froze there and her eyes grew big,

"What the…"

I thought Bree was messing with me as a nameless being drew her in.

"June!" Her arm disappeared into the fall, as if it was sucked in.

"You play too much!" I rolled my eyes.

But her eyes said she wasn't. She reached for me, and I grabbed onto her arm. Like being sucked into a vacuum, we were pulled through to the other side of the waterfall. I held on tight as a gust of wind enveloped us, surrounding us in pitch black. The black grew brighter, into a vivid red and then a luminous yellow.

I gasped as we floated in front of hundreds of light beams, like small floating stars. The flames grew more visible and started to have faces and bodies, like fairies. As soon as I tried to reach for the small figures, a swift and shuddering resistance hit me. We began moving backwards, rewinding out of the vortex. Abruptly we were thrust out of the waterfall, onto the muddy bank. I sat on the ground, stunned and unmoving, eyes frozen on my dry gray jeans. Not a stitch of my clothes was wet anymore, and Bree was fully clothed.

Bree moved her mouth then, but I heard no words. She started to pace around, her mouth still moving, and her gesturing wildly.

Like the volume was slowly being turned up, Bree urged me to get up, "What's wrong with you? C'mon!"

My legs wouldn't move. I stared at the waterfall, looking for any remnants of what we'd just experienced. Nothing. It looked so normal, so innocent.

Bree pulled at me, "We have to leave. June! The fuck are you doing? Let's go."

Feeling slowly returned to my legs. I let Bree haul me up, and we started to walk away. At least that's what my body was doing, but my mind—my spirit—wouldn't leave the fall.

Bree moved much quicker than I could manage, her strides long and shoulders tight. She muttered to herself in front of me, perplexed as she dragged me away from the lake. I was overcome with adrenaline that I couldn't actually apply to anything. So instead, my eyes were twitching, and I felt fidgety. I knew I'd just experienced something that I'd been waiting for all of my life, but I wasn't quite sure what it was. I decided all I cared about was finding out.

Auntie Elaine and Dad greeted us and joked about how short our little excursion was. They decided they were done for the day, and Bree and I helped them pack in silence. On the way home, I was too awestruck to join in on their conversation on the evolution of cell phones.

I ran through each moment, all of which were still so vivid in my mind. Bree plunging into the fall, the vortex opening—None of it scared me. And it should have. I was the girl who'd never veered away from my mom at the grocery story as a kid, because my number-one priority at seven was avoiding "stranger danger." I'd always been cautious, always been safe. Yet, I wasn't scared of what was the most unsafe thing I'd ever encountered. I needed to go back. Things had been weird since I got to North Carolina, but I was tired downplaying it. I wanted answers.

Chapter Four

"When are we leaving?" Bree asked, as she made her way into the kitchen.

Marci bounced in a dining chair twice her size, while munching on a carrot. She looked like a bunny with an afro.

"In a few. Once I finish with this list." Aunt Elaine scribbled thoughtfully in a notepad. "Do we have any more flour? We do." She crossed something out on a notepad. "I think you're gonna like EeBee Day, June. We always have a good time. Isn't that right, Marci?"

Marci bounced and threw her carrot on the ground.

Auntie Elaine told us how she started the monthly tradition to bond better with Bree a few years ago. Hence the name EeBee, for Elaine and Bree. According to my calculations, that meant the custom began around the same time Bree started vandalizing the town.

My mom came into the kitchen, yawning, with her blue tote over her shoulder. "We're going to have so much fun!" She smiled.

She looked like she hadn't gotten much sleep. Part of me wanted to hug her, but the part of me that couldn't think of hugging her without wanting to cry.

In spite of the cheesy name, I was looking forward to EeBee Day. It reminded me of my grandma's tradition of going to a movie with me and my mom each month. We'd only ever watch movies starring women, and they had to have at least one black person in a starring role. Those were my grandma's rules, because she "wasn't about to waste a dime on some white nonsense." Some months when no movies fit our criteria, we'd have a movie night at home. The last month we ever did it, we saw *Eve's Bayou*.

Auntie searched the cabinet and crossed out something else."I suppose I'm gonna need to change the name soon, since Marci's getting older. Marci, you gotta help me think of a new name, babe!"

Bree rolled her eyes. We hadn't talked much since the whole waterfall thing the day before. I'd tried to talk to her about it that night, and she shut me out.

"Just don't, okay?" she said. And would say again the next two times I brought it up.

I couldn't just let it go, though. I had to talk to her, I just had to figure out how. I had every intention of going back to that waterfall, and an even stronger feeling that she needed to be with me to make whatever happened happen again.

We hopped into the Ford van and headed for Gordon, the closest "big city" to the McKinneys' farm. The space between homes shrunk the closer we got, until each house was adjoined to the next. Open fields and dusty roads were replaced by smooth pavement and quirky local shops with names like Rocks Clocks. The roads were narrower than back home and the buildings shorter. In front of us was a town square, surrounded by patches of lawn filled with shrubbery and a few statues on the grassy spaces between streets. In the center of the square were dozens of tents, and it dawned on me that we were going to an outdoor market. I saw signs for jewelry and clothing, fruits and veggies, toys and trinkets.

Auntie grinned back at me and Bree, "We're here."

We managed to park in a narrow alley at the outskirts of the brimming activity. Mom and Auntie moved slowly, comfortably. Their pace made me anxious, or maybe I just noticed how anxious I was the more relaxed they seemed. I was starting to hate how oblivious everyone else was to how strange my trip had been. I was alone, even with Bree moving just as rigidly as I was. I wish I knew what she was thinking.

Auntie led as we navigated past a crowd of locals on a cobblestone path. On either side of us were squat street lamps, surrounded by shrubbery and freshly cut grass, all leading to the market. I allowed myself to float to the back of the crowd behind Mom and Bree and everyone, until I was lagging behind on my own.

As I passed by, one of the lamps caught my eye. A woman in Lululemon pants power walked past me, and I shuddered as she froze in place. The street lamp flickered, softly at first, then brighter, until the light sparked and popped right in front of me. The beacon of light left the fixture and continued to grow.

Unlike the times before, this all was familiar to me now. I focused intently, hoping for clues. The light molded from a ball into a figure with arms and legs.

"Oh my god." I said, my voice barely above a whisper.

Everything but the light was frozen in time. The ethereal figure's feet floated just above where the lamp once stood.

"*Juniper,*" spoke a familiar voice.

With its arms outstretched, and a face soft and feminine, it said, "*You must return to Cantatis.*"

I pushed out a squeaky, "Cantatis?"

"*You are needed. Return with Breana. We will be waiting for you.*"

The figure slowly floated away, its eyes once bright, quickly fading.

"Wait!" I pleaded to the figure. But whatever spirit was there left anyway.

I stood, paralyzed, as the world around me came roaring back to life. The power walker made her way past me, like a street lamp hadn't just exploded behind her. I started walking again to catch up with everyone.

"Girl. You are so weird, what are you doing?" Bree made her way back to me.

"We need to talk about the waterfall . . . thing," I stared her square in the eyes.

"Whoa, okay. Chill. And, like I said, no." She laughed, starting to walk away from me.

"Look. I don't have time to joke around with you," my assertion surprised even me.

She halted mid-step and swiveled around. Mom, Marci, and Auntie had stopped at a fruit stand just within sight, and just out of earshot. I made sure of it. I didn't know how secretive this needed to be, but I was surely getting confidential vibes.

She gritted her teeth and said, low clipped tone, "I'm not going back. So before you ask me again, don't."

It was like I'd just been reprimanded by my mom. The sternness in her voice pierced me, but I tried not to show it. I think she thought I was done after that, but little did she know I wasn't deterred, just postponed. As far as I was concerned, my new life mission was to figure out what was at that waterfall, and I wasn't about to let Breana

McKinney stop me. But I still let her walk away. I knew I had to convince her, but the truth is, I had no idea how.

I joined everyone at the farmers market.

Auntie sniffed a candle, "Oh, nice. I like that. Smell."

She handed the candle to my mom.

"Wow, a tad minty. Very nice." Mom said.

"Reminds me of my ma's perfume. It's lovely, right?" Auntie asked.

Still pondering how I would convince Bree, I floated along behind everyone as we walked past a donut stand and a knitting station. I caught snippets of Auntie's story about her mother, a Jamaican immigrant, who lived with Aunt Elaine's older sister in Tennessee. Auntie trailed off in the middle of her monologue, as if she regretted talking about it, but continued when Mom insisted. Mom's smile seemed sincere. Maybe it comforted her. Maybe it made her feel closer to Grandma. Or maybe nothing could help her feel closer to Grandma, but she wanted to revel in someone else's love for their mother.

I let my mind circle back to the figure I just saw. I felt confusion and anxiety clouded my mind as the words—*You must return. You must return. Return. Return*—replayed in my head.

I grew frustrated. How could anyone experience what Bree and I had and not want to learn more about what happened? It didn't make sense to me, and I refused to accept that she just "didn't want to." I gathered my nerves and marched up to Bree, ready to argue.

"Bree—" I started.

"You wanna look around?" she interrupted, without even looking my way.

I followed her gaze to a tall guy with dark, shaggy hair and a strawberry blonde-haired girl dressed in black combat boots outside of a busy little cafe. They looked our age, and both held skateboards.

I watched just long enough to catch the guy mouth to Bree, "C'mon," while both he and the girl gestured at the same time.

I wasn't fooled. I knew Bree only wanted me to come along to get to these two, but I didn't care. Even if her offer was total bullshit, this would give me more time to talk her into going back to Cantatis with me.

So I said, "Yeah, ok. If you promise to at least talk to me about the waterfall."

She rolled her eyes. "Fine. Whatever," and huffed away.

I'm not really sure if she heard anything beyond "Yeah," but I decided to take the chance. The stakes were high, and I had no time to waste. Bree strolled over to an organic toiletry booth, where Auntie, Mom, and Marci were smelling floral soaps.

Bree wrapped her arm around Auntie and gave the most drawn-out "Maaaaaa" in human history.

"Yes?" Auntie replied.

Bree sweetly responded, "You mind if I show Juniper around?"

"Well…" Aunt Elaine breathed in a lavender body wash, "You don't wanna hang out here?"

"June really wants to check out the cafe."

She pointed to the cafe where that elusive duo had mysteriously disappeared. I nodded. I lied.

"If Vivian's all right with it, I suppose that's fine," she said.

Mom, more on the upside than she had been in months, smiled and said, "Fine with me."

I felt bad that I was lying to her. But I reminded myself of my mission and decided I was doing what had to be done.

Bree thanked and kissed her mom on the cheek. Seriously, I never thought I'd see Bree act so sugary sweet to anyone.

"Be back in an hour!" Auntie called after us as we crossed the street.

Yeah, I wasn't really jumping in excitement to hang with my newfound nemesis. But if I'm being totally real . . . I was sort of, kind of, intrigued by Bree's two mysterious friends. They clearly had the same IDGAF, chill demeanor as Bree, but since they weren't her, I was optimistic about how that would translate. And I was about to hang out with people my own age. A thing I often either avoided or didn't really get the chance to do. I was starting to itch.

Bree kept glancing back at Mom and Aunt Elaine. When we reached the other side of the street, she shot her friends a nod and headed into the cafe.

The old, grey stone exterior contrasted the modern look of the bistro indoors. The walls were dark blue, accented with espresso-stained mahogany floors, black bistro tables and chairs, an inky chalkboard boasting the entire menu in neat handwriting, and modern, black hanging lamps. The baristas wore all black, and the person directly behind the counter donned thick rings of black eyeliner around their deep brown eyes.

Of course this is the place Bree would meet her friends.

"Bree!" A girl with strawberry blonde hair and a sprite-like voice jolted me out of my thoughts.

"Vera!" Bree cooed back.

Soft and pale, with hands like cherubs, the only characteristic we shared was our height. She wore dramatic black lipstick over heart-shaped lips and taupe eye shadow around her starry-blue eyes. She squeezed Bree so tight that when she let go, some of the glitter on her face had transferred to Bree's Pink Floyd tank top.

Slightly behind Vera was the guy I saw outside, only now I wasn't so sure if "he" was a "he" at all. They were lanky and androgynous, with baggy jeans, a ratty old hoodie, and a face so stunning and delicate I couldn't stop staring.

"How the hell did you get out of your jail cell?" they asked in a voice like a cello.

Bree punched their arm in a joking way and said, "Fuck you, my mom let us go."

Up to this point, I'd stood in the background like a ghost. I was used to disappearing, so I didn't even think to introduce myself, until Bree said "us" and reminded me I was technically her guest.

Bree gestured toward me, "Juniper, this is Sen. She's an asshole."

Sen shook my hand, and I held on longer than a normal person should. My sweaty palms got sweatier by the second. But in spite of the sweat, I got chills. I let go in what I hoped was enough time to redeem myself. I spent the next few seconds finding new and creative ways to stare at Sen without being creepy. Something about her evident confidence, or that jawline, or those deep, chestnut-brown eyes—

"And this is Vera."

I forced my gaze to a far less mesmerizing Vera standing next to me.

"Bree, we know Juniper! You told us already, remember?" Vera giggled, her sparkly bracelet glinting. I studied at Bree, searching for what she might have told them.

Vera continued, "You're the space girl from New York, right?"

"Uh…" I really didn't know how to respond to that. Did she call me that it because I went to space camp? Or because I want to be a cosmologist? Or because I'm weird? I wasn't sure.

"Yep, that's her," Bree confirmed.

I know being a nerd or a geek or whatever is supposed to be trendy now, but in moments like those—it never feels like it. And maybe it's just the case that adults can be cool nerds, but kids and teens can't be. Maybe one day, when I'm twenty, I'll proudly call myself a nerd. But then, that particular day—the word felt like a slur.

"June, how you liking Evershire so far? Or in your case, Bree's dungeon?" Sen blessed the world with her words. I laughed at the thought of Bree living in a dungeon and said,

"I like what I've seen so far, I guess."

I worried she'd know that I was talking about her in my mind and averted my eyes. I wondered how I might manage to flirt with her. *I*, Juniper Bray, was worried about flirting with someone.

After a little more small talk that thankfully didn't center around me, Vera made her way up the line and ordered a black coffee. The barista complimented her tutu, and she curtsied. This odd, modern teen world was almost more bizarre than the thought of Cantatis.

"Thank you very much!" she squealed.

She grabbed her coffee and nearly strutted right past us, leading the way out the door. She was petite, but knew how to get your attention. Everyone filed out after her. I followed behind, still enchanted by Sen, who'd just placed her hoodie over her shaggy dark bob. No one person had ever captured my attention like she did. I was enthralled.

As we walked, they chatted amongst themselves without indicating their plans. I hesitated to ask where we were going, not wanting to reinforce the stiff reputation Bree probably already instilled in their minds. Finally, after walking for several minutes, my curiosity conquered my nerves.

"Where are we going exactly?" *Casual enough*, I thought.

Sen looked back at me and flashed a devilish grin that made my heart skip a beat. "Just a little place we like to call 'The Hole.'"

I sped up, trotting a little to catch up to Sen's long strides. I liked how she towered over me, which isn't difficult seeing that I'm very short. I wanted to know more about her, but in that moment just being beside her was enough.

We walked until we reached the quiet side of town. No more cute shops or farmers markets. Suddenly, Vera stopped short and declared, "We're here!"

In front of us, at the end of a crumbling path, were the bones of an old shop with broken glass windows and a forlorn sign that read "No Trespassers" nailed to the door. I rolled my eyes at how textbook rebellious it would be that we were actually going in there.

From the outside, you could see straight into the shop front. And sure enough, Sen, Bree and Vera expertly made their way around the cracks and small craters in the walkway to the side of the brick building where there was a large enough hole to have once accommodated a door. Three bikes lay in the grass beside the hole and narrow stairs leading down to a cellar door.

Sen looked both ways before crouching in. I heard muted conversations growing louder with each step. The sound of laughter, talking, cursing, and wheels on concrete grew twice as loud once we were inside.

Bree and her friends greeted a sweaty, goofy-looking boy covered in tattoos. Sen immediately started to skate with him. Bree and Vera found a spot on the ground to sit. I did a quick headcount, and there were eight kids present, not including us. Everyone seemed to have that older vibe like Bree, except for me. Three of the kids smoked sitting on upside-down trash cans on the opposite end of the dusty basement. Odd Future played on an IPod in the corner, hooked up to speakers. I sat cross-legged next to Bree, doing my very best performance of relaxation.

"Cool?" Vera reached out a small joint to me.

Thanks to Bree, I actually knew what this meant and quickly said, "No, I'm good."

I tucked my shaky hands under my legs.

Vera shrugged her eyes and kept smoking.

Bree laughed, "June doesn't do fun things."

As much as I'd decided Bree was the worst, I realized in that moment maybe she felt the same way about me. I hated feeling like such a goody two-shoes. I snatched

the joint out of Vera's hand and took a drag. And choked.
Great.

Bree laughed, and I'm pretty sure Vera was giggling
too. Two other nosey guys walked over to see what
happened. Sen came over and patted me on the back, as the
last of the coughs left my body. While I loved having Sen so
close to me, I also wanted to hide under a rock.

"You alright?" Sen asked.

"Yeah," I rasped.

She smiled at me and patted me one more time
before going back to skating.

Sen coasted for bit on her board before returning
and asking, "You skate?"

I shook my head and jumped at Vera screeching,
"We'll teach you!" before I had a chance to even open my
mouth.

Sen was really good. She did a few tricks before
handing me the board, "Here. It's easy. I'll show you."

I stepped on the board, one foot, then the next.

"Okay, now take one foot off and push."

And I did.

"Okay. Just coast."

I "coasted" all the way into the wall, my palms on
concrete saving me from a full-out fall, face-first on the
concrete.

"Not bad!" Sen laughed as she helped me up, then
added, "I've only been skating for, like, two years. I sucked
when I started. You're doing better than I did."

My teeth reveal themselves in spite of myself. Usually I would have been so humiliated. I was a little but was comforted by Sen helping me up.

"You alright?" Sen asked.

I nodded. She continued to help me coast in the basement, but not for long. At least it didn't feel like enough time. I paused for a moment to rest, leaning my hand on the wall, which exposed the time on my watch.

I was swiftly knocked out of my infatuated daze. We'd already been away for almost two hours!

I darted towards Bree and flashed my wrist, "Look!"

Bree's head was covered in a shroud of silver smoke, "And?"

"We're late!" I could feel the panic building in my chest.

"God, chill." She shrugged.

She and Vera giggled, stoned and carefree. I snatched what was left of a joint out of Bree's fingers and handed it to Vera.

"I'm leaving. They're probably looking for us by now."

Tingles rolled down my spine, and I knew I'd be itching soon. I'd never been this sure I'd get in trouble in my entire life. What was I thinking? And I never even mentioned Cantatis. Not once.

Bree just stared at me.

I tried not to look at Sen. I just knew her eyes were on me. I knew if I hadn't been nervous about Mom and

Auntie, I would have been embarrassed. I knew I probably looked like the biggest dweeb to set foot in that basement.

But still, I said, "I'm leaving." and marched hard down the sidewalk. I thought about how horrible Bree had been since the waterfall. I thought she was trying to save face after getting so scared at the vortex with me. A part of me felt a little pride that I, of all people, was less scared than Bree to go on an adventure. I was more scared to see Ma than to go back to Cantatis. I wondered if I was even going the right way.

I made it a few blocks before I heard Bree jogging behind me.

"Gat damn," she groaned, sounding slightly out of breath. I didn't respond. We struggled to find the street where Auntie parked. Long moments passed before I spotted the headlights of the Ford. The sight of Mom and Aunt Elaine, arms folded, made my stomach churn.

"What the hell, Bree? I called you six times!" Auntie's southern accent was sharper than before.

I stepped back behind Bree, as if I'd be invisible then.

"Shit," she fumbled in her pocket and pulled out her outdated flip phone.

"Ma, it was on silent, I swear. I didn't even know you called."

I'd forgotten she even had a phone. Now we were really in trouble.

"Matter of fact, give me that," Auntie snatched the phone right out of Bree's hand, stuffed it in her purse, and stormed into the driver's seat.

Bree slithered into the back of the van. She was definitely still high.

Mom shook her head and turned to me, "Where did you two go? You were supposed to be back one hour ago."

"I know. I'm sorry…"

I didn't know what else to say. I'd never done something so obviously rebellious. There was no redeeming statement I could make, no excuse. I was reminded why I never did anything wild in the first place. I was too afraid of the consequences.

Her mom chimed in, far less calm than mine, "You know what, that's a good question, Bree. What were ya'll even up to that would cause you to float your lil tails over here nearly two hours later?"

"I was showing June around, like I said—" Bree started.

Auntie swiveled around to look at Bree. "You were with them lil kids, weren't you? Don't answer. I already know. *And* you're high! Child. You don't even want to know what… I…"

Auntie trailed off and rubbed her temples. Bree's eyes were bloodshot, her expression sheepish. I put my head down. I was glad I'd choked on the little bit of weed I'd tried.

We sat in silence all the way back. I wasn't sure if I preferred that or to hear more from Mom. Her silence was almost deadly. Any time I got in trouble, my mom would go on rants that lasted forever. This whole silent treatment was like torture for me.

When we rolled into the farm, Auntie Elaine unbuckled little Marci from her car seat, who had somehow slept the whole way back.

"Get out of my face. I can't even look at you right now. We'll talk about this later," Auntie said, while pulling half-asleep Marci from her car seat.

Bree and I walked into the house, followed closely by our mothers. I felt like I was walking into a dungeon. I stood in the entryway, shuffling my feet, not sure whether to go upstairs or just stand there with my head down.

Finally I said, "I've gotta go to the bathroom," and started to climb.

"Juniper..." My mom stopped me.

I had a feeling I wouldn't get away. Bree had almost made it to the room. I envied her. Auntie walked away with Marci, mumbling something to herself all the way down the hall.

Mom trapped me with a probing gaze and asked, "What were you two up to?"

A loaded question. I fidgeted with my clothes, trying to figure out what to say. I could tell her the truth. I could just say what actually happened, because I didn't do anything that outrageous, or at least I didn't think so. But I lied.

"We just walked around and lost track of time. We didn't hear Bree's phone; I forgot she even had one! I'm sorry."

I didn't need to lie for Bree about her friends, and I wasn't sure why I did.

Mom's arms were folded, her expression tight, and I couldn't tell what she was thinking, so I kept talking.

"Mom, we didn't mean to be late, really."

She shook her head and threw up her hands, "I'm tired, June. I'm not sure what's gotten into you but this is ridiculous. I want to trust you but this is just not like you. You know what? I've been sitting in a van for too long, and I'm tired. I am so, very tired. I'm going to call it a day. I suggest you do, too."

And with that, she waved me away.

I went upstairs, dwelling on my mother's disappointment. I opened the bedroom door and was overwhelmed by a bright orb of light at the window. Bree was backing away from the window, moving closer and closer to me. I knew she saw it, too.

"*Cantatis is waiting,*" its voice filled the room, gruff and mysterious, entirely different from the voice I'd heard in the city.

Bree tripped on something, as she stepped back and fell at my feet. The light disappeared.

"Wh-What was that?" Bree stammered, as she clambered to her feet.

"It's what we need to talk about," I said.

CHAPTER FIVE

"We have to go back. That's what the lights keep saying. We can't keep ignoring all these signs."

Bree wouldn't look at me.
She played with the ruffles on her comforter and said, "We?"

"Yes, we. That's what I've been trying to tell you. I saw a light just like this one at the market yesterday, and in the garden, and on my ride over the first day I got here. It told me that the only way I can go back to wherever that waterfall took us is if you come, too." It was like I'd just relieved myself from carrying a bundle of bricks.

"What if I don't want to go back?" her trembling voice was sobering.

I settled in my seat, unsure how to respond. My heart said we had to go, but I was starting to feel even more alone than before. Not like she hadn't been clear about her disinterest before, but I found it hard to understand how anyone could pass up this opportunity. I found it difficult to empathize with someone whose personality was so bold and reckless.

"I don't get you. How are you more afraid of this than me? You act so tough, like nothing bothers you, but then something real comes along, and you're scared," I said finally.

I expected her to shoot me down with one of her sarcastic responses.

Instead she spoke softly, contemplatively. "That waterfall was weird as hell. All of this is . . . It freaked me out, okay?"

That was the most honest she'd sounded since we met.

"That vortex thing we saw, it's not a part of Earth. It's something else. I don't know what, but it's not this, and I'm not trying to play games with other worlds and shit."

I got up and sat next to her on her bed. "I know. I know you're right, and I know it's weird, but still it felt familiar to me somehow. I've been feeling this strange thing since I got here, like I'm supposed to be doing something major, and I didn't know it would involve you before, but I *know* now. I need you, and I know whatever is over there needs us, too. Both of us."

Bree glanced at me and said, "I've been seeing those guiding light things since you got here, too."

I froze.

She kept going, "I didn't know what the hell they were. I thought I was the only one."

She looked me directly in the eye and croaked, "I can't go back."

My heart sank. "Bree—"

"No, okay?" She cut me off and turned away.

"Fine. Don't. I'll do it alone."

"You literally just said you can't do it alone. Just let it go."

"I don't care. I know what I said, but it can't be the only way. There's gotta be something else. Some kind of loophole. And what do you care, anyway?"

I didn't wait for her to respond before I got up and went downstairs. I knew she was right. I knew the voice wouldn't have told us to go together if it wasn't necessary, but something in me refused to believe Bree, of all people, would stop me. I was determined to go beyond the waterfall, with or without her.

CHAPTER SIX

Bree scowled as she climbed into the van. We were headed back to the worksite soon, and I refused to let her bum me out. I'd dreamed about the waterfall the night before and woke up excited and ready for the day. I battled with doubt, as I worried I wouldn't make it past the waterfall without her, but I wouldn't let her see that.

Of all the days Dad and Auntie could have had a trillion tasks planned for us, it just had to be that day. It was as if they'd reserved all the lengthy lab assistant work from years before just for that sunny morning. Bree and I started out with data entry, but not just simple stuff. No, Dad had apparently just completed 45 tests that confirmed similarities between other plants and the Valeferus. Bree and I had to double-check each test and type every detail on Auntie's laptop and in writing on graph paper. I had done data entry before by my own request for one of my dad's projects, on the proven importance of ferns to mental health. I liked reading about his findings. It made me feel like I was in on some big scientific secret. I would have found this task educationally stimulating had it not been a day I planned to travel into a vortex.

After two hours, and the possible beginning stages of carpal tunnel in my left wrist, we finished, only to hear Auntie say, "Good, now you can photograph these!"

She directed me to a translucent box of dozens of leaves pressed between plastic. Beside it was a digital microscope camera that my dad once described as an "exciting toy for any scientific mind." I was supposed to carefully place each unknown specimen under the microscope, photograph it, and label it. Not complicated, just tedious.

I looked at my watch. We'd planned to stay on site for three hours, and already two had passed. I had to be quick, or I'd never get a chance to go to the fall. I was in the zone. I felt like I was prepping for the biggest race of my life, as I developed a smooth pace for each photo. I didn't know who I'd be letting down if I didn't go to the fall; I just knew I wouldn't be the only one disappointed, and the pressure of that was unshakeable.

"Done!" I jumped up, and my dad met my gaze.

"Did you enter the data on paper?"

Nod.

"Photograph the organisms?"

Nod.

"Clean the pipettes?"

"Uh." I hadn't.

I tried pretending I hadn't heard the question, so I could just disappear into the woods, but I'm a horrible actor so, I opened my mouth to confess. When suddenly the unimaginable happened.

"I'll clean them." *Bree* offered to help *me*.

"Okay, great! That's very nice of you, Bree," Dad said.

Bree's expression was something like a smile only a little more sad.

Dad raised his brow, "Well, that's that, then! Go explore."

As Bree started at her chore I headed into the woods one more time. I glanced back at Bree, who had already begun to clean the equipment. I didn't get why she was doing anything nice for me. It's not like we'd been getting along. It's not like I even liked her.

I focused in on the pathway leading to the waterfall. It sunk in that I'd actually be alone, and my heart dropped. I had no real plan in making the portal I'd seen open again on my own. I wasn't even the one to spark it the first time; Bree was. Would I even be able to summon what had come before?

I finally got to the water. I removed my shoes and felt the damp, cool ground beneath my feet. A warmth enveloped me, and I looked up to find another guiding light shimmering directly in front of me. I breathed a sigh of relief. *It's working*, I thought.

I followed the light towards the waterfall. I had made sure to wear shorts that day, so I would have an easier time wading through the water. I was closer to the light than I'd ever been, so close I reached out to touch it. I continued my steady trek toward the fall more relaxed than before, and I was starting to settle in.

"Juniper!" Bree shouted at me as she burst out from the foliage, frantic and out of breath.

What. The. Actual. Fuck. It was clearly backwards day.

I halted in the water and struggled to get words out, "What . . . why are you—what?"

I could barely speak.

"Just wait, alright?" She wheezed as she skidded over slippery mud and into the water.

My mind went immediately to the site with Dad and Auntie. How did she get away so fast?

I made a second attempt, "How did you—?"

"They think I'm trying to pee. I saw a light again, and it led me here. I'm going with you." She spoke in short bursts, quickly closing the distance between us, as she trudged through water fully clothed.

I grabbed her hand as she stepped over a rockier part of the pool. As soon as we touched, I was speechless.

I imagine it's what astronauts feel like in space, only we didn't need oxygen tanks. We hovered before deep, black nothingness. A nothingness that was more like everything and forever. We were surrounded by darkness, moving in midair as if carried by invisible currents. The pitch-black space brightened into a royal blue, and little dots that looked like stars surrounded us.

Through a little peephole, I saw the fall in front of us, only it shone bright blue and the trees behind it looked like animation. There were creatures moving in the water that looked like dinosaurs. Real, actual dinosaurs. The eyelet grew, revealing the land, everything more vivid and opaque. I could see deep into the forest, and though parts of it were familiar but the little, round, wooden homes built high in the trees were like nothing I'd ever seen before. The void opened to a window twice our size and after suspending us for a moment spit us out, deep into the woods.

I scrambled to get up. I breathed in the brisk floral air. There was something so uncanny about the land. It was as if I were in a more magical version of North Carolina, one select few would ever get to see. Bree, who was still holding my hand, rose with me.

Our feet trampled tender petals as we eased through lush vegetation. In front of us were towering trees with brassy golden bark. Instead of standing tall, each branch leaned, creating perfect crescent shapes. Above us, large splashes of orange and brown wood folded into round cottages nooked in every other tree.

Through the trees, I could tell the sky was a purple-ish hue, like right before dawn, but richer and more encompassing. Groups of little beings gathered as they came out of their strange little homes. The path from before was still there, only this time covered in the purple petals from the trees. Naturally, we followed it.

My gaze was interrupted by a white creature racing past us into the trees. It sported a horn on its forehead. I nearly fell over myself when it clicked that I'd just witnessed an actual, factual unicorn in the flesh. Before I could even grasp the sight of it, four others stampeded past us, like we weren't even there. Did they even see us?

"Did you see..." Bree trailed off.

"Yes," I nodded, like an eager kid.

A rush of excitement flowed through me. Bree and I sprinted into the trees after the unicorns. The trees gave way and enveloped us, making the unicorns disappear from our sight.

Each tree was decorated with curly glass charms. A ravine weaved, trickling through the trees. Docked in the stream were tiny boats, stabilized with anchors like necklace pendants, just waiting for their micro crews to return.

Elsewhere in the stream, frog like creatures rowed a boat the size of a shoebox. Tiny fishing rods were propped at the back. Though I couldn't hear what they were saying, I could see their mandibles moving as they spoke to each other.

My feet sagged into soft, blue-green mosses, thick like a carpet. This land was the perfect place to be barefoot.

The frog-looking creatures wore leaf backpacks. The quieter my breath, the more I heard them chatting.

Bree grabbed my arm.

"Did you hear that?" she hissed.

I shushed her, worried we'd scare them away. Bree pulled me behind a tree, where we stumbled and fell, hidden under a tangle of roots.

She scooted closer for a better look, "They may not even speak English."

Feeling bold, I jumped up and shouted, "Excuse me!"

They looked up at me like they were trying to figure out what I was. In unison, they dropped their fishing rods, grabbed their oars, and tried their hardest to row away. As if their tiny little boat could outmaneuver two humans many times their size. It didn't take us long to catch up.

"Wait! I'm not . . . I'm not trying to hurt you or anything! I just—"

They clearly weren't having it. At that point, we were right above them, looking down at the ravine. Under the glittering current, I could see miniature orange fish. The frog things still tried to row away as quickly as they could, but we walked easily beside them. I laughed then; not at them, though. My laugh was like an involuntary reaction to what I'd gotten myself into. I must have been more in disbelief than I even realized. I felt wildly out of my mind.

Bree paused, "Why are you laughing?"

And then she started laughing too, but the creatures weren't amused. One stopped rowing to throw a miniature spear at Bree, which obviously only made me crack up more. At this point I was doubled over, my stomach hurt, and my eyes were starting to water. I didn't even notice when they actually pierced Bree's skin the second time.

She yelled, "Hey!"

Now it was the frogs' turn to laugh.

"No!" She barked like she was punishing a pet.

I could tell they were no longer intimidated by us. Bree and I found refuge behind a tree near the stream, as they kept trying to stab us with their little spears.

I tried again to talk to them, "Please, we don't know where we are. Can you tell us?"

Blank stares.

I tried once more, "Hello? Can. You. Help. Us?" I punctuated each word like an ignorant tourist.

They didn't show any signs of being able to understand, and they were rowing again, though they wouldn't get very far.

I was about to give up, when one of them started pointing beyond the streams, miming something with grand, sweeping movements.

Bree and I carefully hopped over the thin stream. One of the backpacked frogs hopped up on a log beside us and nodded.

A few of the trees there had hollowed windows, with lights glowing through. Then, as I moved in for a closer look, the lights descended all around us and grew so bright I had to look away. Tiny glowing beams perched on the trees, and others fluttered around our heads. Bree and I stood with our backs to each other, surrounded by these flickering beings at every angle. There were more and more by the second, glowing, floating. Then, the flickering grew more rapid, and they began to change.

They were no longer those familiar light beams, but now grey creatures with recognizable wings, and bodies like insects, with muted, human-like faces, no bigger than my hand. Some looked older, others younger, some even like children.

The crowd of them suspended at our eye level parted, creating a narrow pathway in midair, and down came one of them, bigger than the others, with an oval, deep grey face and stunning violet eyes. A crown of twigs sat on her head, and she wore a golden leaf draped into the most elegant gown. She floated at eye level and bowed subtly. On cue, the others bowed deeply around us, too. It was immediately clear to me that she was in charge.

Bree squeezed my hand, and I squeezed hers back, as if to say, "I know, right?!"

"Well, it's about time," said the regal creature.

Her voice was stronger than anything I'd expect from such a tiny figure. I was in such shock that I felt like my vocal chords were out of commission. My mouth hung open like a fly trap, and the rest of me was utterly still.

"About time?" Bree muttered almost inaudibly, but they heard her, anyway.

Their laughter, like the plucking of thousands of violins, crescendoed instantly then dissipated, as if absorbed by the forest. I glanced at Bree, then at the creatures and back.

This is definitely happening. This is real, I thought to myself.

"Come," the majestic creature instructed, and we followed as she floated to a grassy clearing surrounded by trees.

It was the perfect size for hundreds of fairies, but only just big enough for Bree and me to barely move around. The others encircled us, and she drifted beside me. The irises of her violet eyes began to glow a deep gold. I was mesmerized. She nodded to me, and I bowed my head like I was standing before royalty. It wasn't even on purpose, something about her just demanded that response.

The creatures exuded a sense of contagious calm. I wasn't afraid, not even when the ground beneath me began to shift and separate. The glowing being floated backwards, and the grassy circle began to spin and levitate.

Bree and I hovered a foot off the ground.

"Please, sit," she ordered.

We did as instructed and settled inside the circle, our legs dangling over the edge. The space where our patch of ground had been was replaced with a rippling surface that mirrored our reflections. Our images faded, and a familiar face came into view: my grandmother. She was so young I only recognized her from the few photos she'd shown me before.

The purple-eyed fairy began, "Juniper, you have always questioned what's beyond your world."

I nodded without even meaning to. I was staring at the queenly creature like she held the answer to my future, because I truly believed she did.

She continued, "You've always known there was more. The world is not what many think it is. There are other realms, thousands. You see, the stories you once heard from your grandmother, of fairies and mystical creatures, were not imaginary tales. They were memories."

"How—?"

Every word she said resonated with me, yet I struggled with disbelief. Hearing her tell me my grandma's stories were real out loud was too much, like being washed over by waves in a high tide. I didn't know how to feel, or if it was even only one feeling. My logical brain rejected what my heart knew to be true. A moving image like a film of my young grandmother played among the fairy-like creatures in the rippling water below. It was like watching her magical stories come to life. Everything she said, right in front of me.

"There are worlds for creatures you've been told were unreal. The unicorns you saw, the froglets, us. Many of us have tried our time on Earth and have been rejected or endangered. And that is why we have other realms in and around Earth to keep us all safe. You are now in Cantatis, an alternate reality of Earth for beings like ourselves."

The Purple Fairy floated back to join the rest. "Now, to introduce myself: I am Harmonia, Freedom Guide of Cantatis, and we are what humans call fairies. Your grandmother was born with a gift which gives powers that are unimaginable to most. With her gift, she helped protect us and her fellow humans, and in turn we helped protect Earth from those planets and worlds that aren't so kind. You are here because you too, Juniper, have inherited that gift. You are a born Earth Ambassador."

"I don't . . . it doesn't..." I stuttered.

My mind crowded with flashbacks of Grandma's stories, the guiding lights I'd seen since arriving in Evershire, the talking pig. I always knew there was something more, but this was beyond what I could have even dreamed. Bree squeezed my hand again. She hadn't closed her mouth since Harmonia began to speak.

"Now, Breana. You are Juniper's telestic warrior: someone to share her journey, to go into battle with and be Juniper's support through it all. Every ambassador must have one, and you must never speak of this with anyone else."

My stomach churned. I was barely starting to tolerate Bree, let alone like her. She let go of my hand, and I figured she was thinking the same thing.

Harmonia moved closer to us again and spoke with a deeper tone than before. "I must be very clear. Speaking of us or the other realms with anyone else unlocks portals only few should have access to. Speaking of any of this beyond yourselves will cause serious turmoil for all of us. Do you understand?"

I nodded, "Why now? And Bree? I don't . . . It just—"

Bree still hadn't said one word since Harmonia opened her mouth. I couldn't tell what was going on behind her stoic expression.

"You'll learn everything in due time," Harmonia reassured me. "Now, I brought you here today, because there is an emergency in Cantatis. The very thing I told you not to do, another has done. A former Ambassador has betrayed us and told someone about our porthole. We're not sure whom or how, but we do know that someone has been poisoning our elders. No one in Cantatis would do such a thing. We need your help to bring one of our elders back to health."

"Wait! Wait a second . . . I mean what if . . . what if I don't want to do this? You didn't even give me a chance to say what I want!"

I felt like I was watching myself speak. I was out of my body and present and scared, all at once.

"Juniper. If you want to leave now and forget this mission and others to come, you are welcome to do so," Harmonia said calmly. "You have no obligations here and we may appoint a new Ambassador in time. But also, you must remember that we are all connected, whether you want that or not."

Bree cut through her silence with a quivering voice, "What do you mean 'we're all connected'?"

Harmonia said, "If you choose to discontinue your appointed journey as Ambassador of the Earth and telestic warrior, the balance of our realms, our worlds, is uncertain at best. I don't mean to scare you, but the future is bleak without an Ambassador."

Bree wrung her hands.

"This is too much." She mumbled.

I was sweating with nervous energy. I didn't know what to say. Here it was, the magic I'd been searching for all my life. What do you do when your wildest dreams are right in front of you, but you don't feel ready or worthy?

I listened with my head down as Harmonia continued, "I understand if you feel this has all been thrust upon you. Your grandmother had the same fears as a young girl, and like her, you can overcome them. We're all here for you, to help guide you and Breana. And Breana, your heart is strong, and your loyalty truer than any. You must know you are both meant to be here in this moment, if you leave here knowing nothing else."

You are both meant to be here in this moment.
You are both meant to be here.

Harmonia's words played in my head like a song. My truth, that I wanted this, was suffocating under a cloud of self-doubt I couldn't seem to shake. Even if I wouldn't have been able to talk to my grandmother about being an Ambassador, just having her in my life would have made me feel strong enough. I wasn't daring or brave or outspoken like she was—not in the way I needed to be.

A gust of wind circled us and snapped me out of my pity party. The earth beneath our hovering feet began to shake and so did my hands, with fear. I felt useless as Bree fell into the earth, while I kept floating above. I'll never forget how her voice echoed into the trees when she screamed. Harmonia shot a light beam that turned into a glowing rope, and Bree, who was several feet down the rift that'd formed between us, grabbed it. I fell then on level ground and the rope pulled her up to me.

"Run!" One of the fairies said, and we did.

The ground around us crumbled like a fragile piece of paper mache, and with every step, I worried I would go under with it. I ran like my life depended on it, with Harmonia flying in front of us and urging us to hurry. Bree was moving slower so I grabbed her hand and pulled her forward. We ran until the sound of deteriorating land was replaced by water. In the distance, we could see calm waves lapping a lavender shore.

"Follow me," Harmonia demanded.

The briny scent of the sea swept through my senses. The sand, like powdered silver, reminded me of the "silver dust" my grandma used to tell me about in her stories. I remembered how she had the most masterful way of spinning tales without telling me specifically about this magical place. She must have known I'd be here one day. The crests of the waves were a delicate purple that crashed into deeper hues, and somehow any wariness I was feeling turned into awe. Bree covered her mouth, as two unicorns galloped past us like it was no big deal.

"Wow." Bree whispered.

"We're safe. For now. But not for long." Harmonia's tone was somber and cautious.

"What was that?" I blurted.

"Cantatis is no longer as safe as it once was. That is partly why you've been summoned now, of all moments in time. We're in danger, Juniper. All of us."

"I feel like you high-key glazed over this point," Bree said through gritted teeth.

She tapped her foot anxiously, her eyes watering.

"I'd planned to tell you before you left, but we weren't expecting such an interruption. Cantatis has been invaded. Many of our oases have, though these intruders haven't revealed themselves yet. They have attacked our vortexes twice already, which means they have access to, well, anywhere."

"But why? What do they want, other than just tearing everything apart?" Bree asked.

"We're not quite sure, but it seems with all the ambushes as of late, their goal may be to conquer our lands. That's exactly why we need your help. These creatures have already destroyed our sister oasis, Boros, and now they are here. We can only suspect that the Earth is next. We're finding it very difficult to stop them on our own."

"What can we do though?"

I was so confused. I was useless. They had to have called on the wrong person.

"Oh, Juniper, you'll soon know the power you possess. We will train you both, but I assure you, your powers are vast, and once understood, you may truly save us all."

So now I have legit magical powers? If I were in a 1940's drama movie, I probably would have fainted right then. I was overwhelmed with information.

Harmonia went on, "If you so choose, your training will begin posthaste. There's not much time before these creatures start their next phase in Cantatis."

"Which is…?" Bree looked angry now.

I seemed angry enough for the both of us.

"Well, if they deem us worthy, they will likely conquer us all. And if we are not, well, they will destroy us."

Here I was racing through the five stages of mourning, jumping from denial and depression all the way to acceptance. It's like something clicked in me. I wasn't even being dramatic to say the world was on my shoulders. And how could I say no to that? Not even out of guilt, but out of love. I loved my mom and my dad more than anything. I loved my grandma, who'd fought this very same cause. How could I not continue her legacy?

Don't get me wrong, I still didn't think I could handle it. And the thought of dying for all of this wasn't even fathomable for me. Not even a little bit. But I knew in that moment that I couldn't run away from this. I had to try; it's what my grandma would have wanted. Bree's arms were folded, and her face glowed red like there were lights behind her cheeks. She must have still been in the denial stage.

"Now, if you choose to join us, I will give you your first task. But only if you choose."

She hovered there in front of us with what looked like fairy guards. Behind her, the lavender ocean was flowing, beautiful, unbothered by all the thoughts swirling around in my brain.

"I'll do it."

I snapped my head to the side to find Bree, arms down, deliberate, stepping forward. I was shook.
It took me a moment to catch my breath before I said, "Yes, me too."

Harmonia's round, purple face beamed. She nodded and simply said, "Good," and pride enveloped me.

Then she said, "Stay back for a moment. Wahlil may be gentle, but he's quite large."

I stepped back, as the waves grew in front of me. Harmonia flapped her wings, spreading them wider and wider, until they were much longer across than Bree was tall. She opened her mouth to speak, but instead of words, she let out a howl that echoed out over the waves.

As the noise grew, the waves swelled, until something broke the surface. A smooth-backed creature like a whale, but much, much larger, gracefully rose out of the water. Out came a head disproportionately small for its body and a long neck that rivaled any giraffe's. Its eyes were like shiny coal, and its body the color of cool steel.

Harmonia turned to us, "You may recognize Wahlil from the Loch Ness Monster myth of Scotland. As you've probably guessed, it's no myth."

Wahlil snuffled, sending silver dust through the air.

"He's not too fond of the myth. How are you feeling, Wahlil?"

He shook his head and moaned again, his body slumping toward the shore.

Harmonia fluttered over to us. "These creatures causing havoc in our lands make sure to attack our elders first. They've made them sick, and Wahlil, being our eldest, is hurt the most. We must save him for when we eventually face these horrible beasts. Wahlil's powers will greatly benefit us by helping shield our portals, but only if he is strong enough. So, some herbs are only available on Earth, just like we have some only available to us here. We've tried everything here, and it just won't do. The only thing that can save him now is an agrimony plant from your land that we call Velvet's Ear. We know you have it in your garden, Bree. We fairies can only go to Earth in spirit form. We cannot bring any earthly things with us on our return journeys. And one more thing: Only an Earth Ambassador can bless the plant to heal Wahlil. That's where you come in, Juniper."

I took a moment to absorb her words then asked, "How long do we have?"

"We only have a short window to guarantee Wahlil can be healed, and he's deteriorating quickly. You must arrive here at sundown Earth time tomorrow and must return with Velvet Ear. But you must bless it before you arrive, which requires a few special words and movements. And keep in mind, once you accept this task and return to Earth you will lose a bit of time as the universe shifts to accept you as our new Ambassador. This will only happen once as usually time stops when you teleport here, but if you cannot make up for the time change this time this will all be for naught."

"So we gotta chant like witches to save a dying loch ness monster before our time runs out?" Bree laughed.

"Essentially, yes," Harmonia responded swiftly.

"Oh." Bree stopped laughing.

"Listen. When you've found the Velvet's Ear, you must say Wahlil's name seven times while holding it between you. Then you will both hold one piece of the herb between you and circle around seven times as well. Can you do this, girls?"

I nodded. I nudged Bree, and she shrugged reluctantly.

"Good. Now go." Harmonia began to disappear, her body fading on the wind.

"Wait!" I cried.

"We don't go with my dad tomorrow to the forest! How are we supposed to get back here?"

Still fading, she said, "Trust yourselves. You'll find a way."

She disappeared into thin air, leaving us alone on the quiet lavender beach. I had just one second of panic, before a spark appeared before us, and everything went black.

Chapter Seven

I squinted at tinted blue skies through lace curtains. My watch said 6 p.m. on the dot, just one and half hours before sundown when we'd need to be back at Cantatis, and I had no memory of how I'd even made it into my bed. We'd lost so much time just like Harmonia said.

"Bree," I whispered. "Bree!"

She groaned.

"Bree!"

She jerked her covers away, hard enough to throw herself onto the floor. Frustration and grogginess battled on her face.

She said, "Shit!" then wiped the sleep out of her eyes.

I changed into overalls like the outfit I had was on fire. I ran downstairs without waiting.

"C'mon!" I whispered, as if anyone but us would be asleep this late in the evening.

I ran straight to the garden, not even considering the fact that I had no idea what agrimony looked like. It was one of the few plants I'd never seen my grandma use. I heard Bree stumbling behind me with heavy feet, panting.

She muttered something with her hands stuffed in pajama pockets.

"What?" My eyes darted around, unsure how to even begin.

"I said what the fuck does agrimony look like?"

My heart began to race.

"If you don't know *and* I don't know, how are we supposed to do this?" I felt myself starting to panic.

Bree laughed, "Girl. You ever hear of Google?"

We jogged inside and into the living room, where an old Apple desktop computer sat on a red, wooden desk in front of the window. It took a good five minutes to boot.

Bree clicked into the Google homepage and typed in "Agrimony." And we waited. And waited. And precious moments passed, as the buffering spin wheel taunted us before we finally admitted defeat.

"What the fuck?" I whispered, frustrated enough to actually curse.

Bree shrugged, "It works most of the time. Or like, half the time."

I cocked my head at her and she clarified, "We live in the country. What do you expect?"

Sure, we still had time, but my anxiety was starting to take over anyway.

Bree seemed to sense it, because she nudged me, "We can just ask my dad."

"What if he asks us why we want agrimony? What do we say then?" I folded my arms and hid my sweaty palms.

"Chill. I'll figure it out in the moment—"

I cut her off there, "In the moment!"

"June! I swear he'll just be happy we're talking."

I was silent for a moment. I usually don't care for spontaneity, but for some odd reason, I accepted her response.

Still skeptical, I nodded, "Okay. Fine."

I heard the faint sounds of Earth, Wind & Fire coming from the kitchen. Bree led the way, and we were met with a cheerful Uncle Robbie, bobbing his head while cutting red peppers at the table.

"Hey, Dad," She bellowed.

He whirled his head up, surprised, "Finally up, I see! How y'all doin'?"

I laughed like someone who wasn't hiding anything.

"Yeah, been so tired from helping on the site, I guess," I lied.

I wasn't remotely tired. I was a fully charged Duracell battery.

"We're good." Bree chirped, just as shady as ever, "Actually, I wanted to ask you —"

"Oh! I forgot to tell y'all," Uncle dawdled on over to the top of the fridge and reached for a bowl of sweet potatoes, "I'm making your favorite tonight, with a twist. Gonna give a few to the neighbors, let 'em test it out."

He set the bowl on the table and went right back to cutting. I hoped he wasn't implying what I thought he was implying.

"Uh," I looked at my watch.

We had about an hour left. Bree shot me this defeated look and slumped into the seat beside me.

I needed some sort of plan. Maybe an hour seems like a lot to you, but in my mind it was just a hop, skip, and a jump too short for margin of error, aka hanging out with a guy who loved to talk as much as Uncle Robbie.

I took a seat.

There were exactly 14 sweet potatoes, and two knives. Seven each, and then we could go. Just seven. I started peeling, and it got quiet. My optimism went up exactly one notch.

But then he quipped, "So what do you enjoy more, working with your dad or on the farm?"

"With my dad, by far."

He burst out laughing and through chuckles said, "Well, that was easy!"

"Dad, you *know* farm work isn't fun," Bree interposed.

"Well, let me tell you something; I'm really happy to see y'all getting along so well. I knew you would!"

Bree rolled her eyes, but she also had an inconspicuous smirk on her face that made me smile a little.

I shrugged. "Yeah, I guess it's all the time we've been spending at the site."

I said site, but I meant waterfall. I really, really wanted to say waterfall.

"I wouldn't doubt it. You know, that's how your dad and Elaine became friends, through science. It's really something. Learning about the world, that sort of curiosity, it really brings people together, you know, 'cause the universe, as you'll find out, is a fascinating place."

"You are so right," Bree said.

"What were you trying to say a minute ago?" asked Uncle Robbie.

Bree answered, "Oh, yeah, uh, we wanted to know what agrimony looks like. Like if you could show us in the garden after this, that'd be dope."

I envied Bree's relaxed delivery.

Uncle perked up with a grin spreading across his face and asked, "Since when've you been interested in little known herbs like agrimony?"

I kept peeling.

"I don't know, it just seems cool, I guess. Like, it's interesting," Bree shrugged at me.

It was the least believable thing she'd said since we'd entered the room. In spite of that fact, Uncle seemed to believe it.

"Well, okay. That's wonderful. Wonderful. Of course I can help. Just give me about an hour to finish up preparing this meal right quick."

I put down my knife. One hour from now, we'd miss our deadline for Cantatis. I darted a look at Bree.

She jumped in, "Well, we were hoping you could pause for a sec and show us after this? Cause we have this pact to like start studying about lab stuff before it gets dark out and really need this part of it to get started."

Wow, this girl was quick on her feet.

I nodded like I really knew what she was talking about, "Yeah, just based on the sunlight and stuff, we have to be outside at a certain time, and yeah, it's a whole thing."

Who even am I?

"Oh, okay. Okay. Well..." He paused just long enough for me to quietly implode. Finally, he said, "Alright. Finish up the potatoes, and I'll head out there with you."

I took a long breath like I'd been swimming under water too long. Bree kicked my leg under the table, and I glanced up to catch her flashing that signature Cheshire smirk. Peeling potatoes is one of those things that no matter how quickly you want to finish, it'll always disappoint you how slow you have to go. On my very last one, I jumped up and finished while standing, I was so eager to get out.

"Y'all ready?"

I nodded and wiped my hands on my jeans. We filed out the door, like a duck and its babies through a pond. Twenty minutes. Some of our lost time was due to Uncle Robbie telling us a story about the time he lived in Los Angeles right after he graduated high school with dreams of becoming an actor. After every long pause he took I grew more and more anxious. I felt like someone was having a jam session on my chest.

"Okay now, one thing you should know about agrimony is it's always gonna look a little ashy, like somebody threw some baby powder on it and forgot to rub it in."

Uncle Robbie chuckled to himself like he'd told the greatest joke. He knelt down, surrounded by plants, and wafted in everything. He pawed at a few herbs, sniffing them tenderly, lingering in each aroma. I folded my arms.

"Y'all should get down here with me, smells a lot richer down here."

And so we did. Now all of us were kneeling down in the midst of beautiful plants.

"Look at that," Uncle pointed to a plant with red flowers. "Came in real nicely. Those are called Rue."

Bree rolled her eyes.

"And now to the main attraction."

Uncle Robbie leaned into a bright green weed with yellow flowers farther back in the garden. He stood up, smelled it, and picked a nice bushel.

"Agrimony."

He handed it to me, pointing down at my nose. It smelled bitter like asparagus.

"You think this is enough?" Bree asked me.

"I guess," I had no idea.

"You need anything else?" Uncle asked. "An herb tour, perhaps?"

He chuckled.

Bree tapped him on the back and said, "That would be everything. Like for real, for real. But can we get a rain check?"

He looked a little upset, but quickly cheered up, "Of course! Know you got some research and science and such to attend to. I won't hold you!"

"Thank you!" I shouted back at him, as he made his way inside.

"Not a problem, lil June!" He still calls me that, ever since that last summer we visited. It makes me smile just thinking about it, cause with that being the first time he'd dubbed me "lil June" it felt a bit out left field. Nowadays he hasn't called me just "June", and if he did *that'd* be weird.

Finally.

"Ok, let's find this porthole," I sounded assertive, but felt mostly worried.

We had exactly 17 minutes. I thought I knew where it would be. I led Bree to the fountain in the garden, where I'd seen the light before, and we waited. I had been so sure a beam would appear and take us where we needed to go, but nothing happened.

"Wait a second. Maybe it takes time," I said, trying to be reassuring.

I circled around the angel statue and down the dirt path towards the vegetable patch.

Still nothing.

Bree sat right in the dirt and glared up at me. She started playing with the grains of her hand. Thirteen minutes. I just knew this was the end. I sat with her, and for a good minute, we were silent.

"When did she die, your grandmother?"

My heart skipped a beat. It's not like I never expected Bree to bring this up, it's just well, I thought it'd at least take her a few months. But alas. My eyes began to water the more I thought of her. I turned away, not wanting Bree to see.

"Two months ago . . . almost three."

I was swimming in memories of my grandma, it's like I wasn't even there anymore. Bree might as well have left me. But she didn't.

"Oh..." was all she managed to say.

She swirled her foot in the mud, and I imagined she felt just as awkward as I did. I'd thought about my grandmother even more since leaving Cantatis. I thought of her being an Ambassador, and I felt with all of my being that she'd want the same for me. This hopeful part of me wished that she was just in another universe somewhere, waiting for me to be strong like her.

"I'm sorry," Bree muttered under her breath, still watching her feet.

"Why?" I was confused.

There were a lot of things she could have apologized for.

"I—I mean, I dunno, it seems like you were close. And after the whole thing with the fairies, I guess, I don't know. She seemed low-key cool."

Not that I would ever think of Bree as any sort of motivator, but hearing her say "cool" in association with my idol was exactly what I needed.

"What the hell." Bree threw up her hands, "I thought maybe talking about her would, like, bring her energy or something. Like maybe she'd help us."

Bree got up and stomped to the pigpen. She paced back and forth beside Wilbur. I reluctantly walked over to her, not sure what else to do.

"Don't fret, girls," little Wilbur said, surprising both of us, even though I knew he could talk.

Bree jumped back, "What the–"

"Hello, Breana. I am from Cantatis. Juniper and I have met."

She stepped back but kept her eyes locked on him.

"You're a pig," Bree struggled to say.

"Yes. Don't be alarmed. Listen. You were where you needed to be. Return to the garden. Be prepared when you go this time, and you will find what you're looking for."

It took me a moment to understand, but then it hit me. We hadn't chanted at all.

"Oh!" I cried.

I hugged Wilbur and ran back to the garden, agrimony in hand. Harmonia's words flowed into my thoughts as if placed there. I spoke them allowed: *Say*

Wahlil's name seven times while holding it between you. Then hold one piece of the herb between you and circle around seven times as well.

Together we chanted, "Wahlil, Wahlil..."

Right then, like a fly at a cookout, Junior traipsed over to us.

He reached for the bushel of agrimony and managed to grab a piece. "Is that a weed? Why y'all playing with weeds?"

Bree swatted his hand away, "Absolutely none of your damn business."

"Imma tell daddy you're playing with his herbs."

And with that, Robbie started for the door.

"Daddy knows we're 'playing with his herbs.' And we're not playing, Robbie, damn. Leave us alone."

We had two minutes.

I had an idea, "I'll give you ten dollars to leave us alone and go back in the house."

Junior tilted his head to the side and smiled like the annoying child that he was.

"Ten just to leave y'all alone?" He squinted his eyes and looked like he thinking very deeply, then eventually said, "Okay!"

Phew.

"I'll give it to you when we come back inside, but you gotta go, like right now."

Junior raced back in so fast he made dust clouds behind him.

Like we'd read each other's minds, we took each other's hands again and started chanting. We circled each other seven times, and the guiding light I'd been hoping for appeared before us like it had always been there, held in place.

We were just an arm's reach away. The portal opened wider, and we were immediately sucked in.

This time, we soared past a golden meadow into the woods, and plopped right onto the silvery sand, close to the water's edge.

In front of us were rich lilac waves and bare sand, but no creatures in sight. Suddenly, the voice of a beautiful soprano, constant and steady, filled my ears. We stepped back to make way for the growing waves in front of us, and out rose giant Wahlil. Around us, fairies revealed themselves from all directions.

And then the source of the high-pitched trill, Harmonia, flew over us. I handed Harmonia the agrimony. She grasped it tightly.

"Once you have completed this mission, once Wahlil is healed, there is no turning back," Harmonia reminded us.

No turning back, I repeated in my head. I mulled it over. I chewing on it like gum. *No turning back. Okay.* I nodded.

Wahlil met us at the shore, a paler and more faded grey than before. With a wave of her hand, Harmonia made the agrimony rise in midair and liquefy. The greenish liquid orbited around us, slowly molding into an orb in the center of us. The concoction floated towards the sea, and Wahlil swallowed it down with pain in his eyes.

The waves went wild, and we ran out of the way before the sea poured over us. His pale grey body darkened into a black charcoal, and his skin looked rejuvenated in a way we hadn't seen the first time we met. His black eyes glistened, and he waved his long neck back and forth, like some sort of dance. He started to glow like the ocean. Letting out a sigh of relief, he turned and swam away into the depths of the lavender sea.

Harmonia fluttered her wings with a small bow and said, "Well done."

Bree's hands were shaking, and I looked down to find mine were, too. A wind surrounded us and pushed us closer, face-to-face. I should have been afraid, but I wasn't.

"Please, clasp hands," Harmonia instructed.

We did. The wind required we stay still, legs stiff as if cemented to the ground. The sand beneath us rose, circling us like a tornado. There was really no turning back now.

Without time for a second thought, Harmonia invoked the words that would bind me to my new interdimensional role:

> *"Of worlds apart, of worlds the same,*
> *Of times unknown, of present plain,*
> *Of future, past, and in between,*
> *Of Juniper and Breana and earthly things.*

You join us now for saving grace.
As Ambassador of the Human Race.
You shall forever be connected,
And we the same to you."

Our feet no longer touched the ground, our skin glowed golden brown from our fingertips, up our arms and shoulders, down our torsos all the way down to our feet.

Harmonia continued, "From now on, Juniper Bray and Breana McKinney, we are forever connected to you."

We floated down again. The light left our toes and floated into space.

We nodded. She continued.

"Now go back, the two of you, to your earthly land. And very soon, my girls, we will meet again."

Our hands repelled like opposing magnets, so strongly they threw us backwards to the ground. When we landed, we were on familiar grass. McKinney grass. It was like we'd never left.

Chapter Eight

With a sinister face, like a blend between a tiger and a wolf, and a thick, raspy voice, Aggro was a more endearing creature than their odd appearance led on. On all fours they were still taller than I was, and their voice, like the strum of an out-of-tune bass, had me really shaken up. Aggro was our trainer, a Beyan, whose species had trained hundreds of Ambassadors before us, one of them being my grandmother. I knew not to fear them, because Harmonia said so, but still found myself intimidated by their . . . well, everything.

Oh, yeah, and Aggro and other Beyans have no gender, no sex. Honestly, Beyans find the fact that humans even care about gender strange.

Aggro once said, "Gender? I cannot fathom such a category."

Bree once asked what pronouns we could use and Aggro explained many past trainees used "they" and "them", so we did, too.

It was our first full day to train with Aggro, and luckily we'd traveled with Dad and Auntie enough to have developed a routine to get us out of our chores real quick. It was strange—we'd have to make it to Cantatis at certain times like at sunset or sunrise, but when we returned to our realm, it was like no time had passed at all.

Harmonia said we had to know the allying worlds as well as we knew our own. She told us that many of the other worlds were just Earth on a different wavelength. We share space with so many other worlds that we can't see, that we run into and pass by and at any given moment may be staring at without even realizing it. She says that's why portholes can so easily connect us. Cantatis is Earth. Earth is Cantatis.

It had been one week since healing Wahlil, and everything was seemingly quiet, but we were promised that wasn't the case. That's where Aggro came in. They'd teach us as much as they could before those creatures corrupting everything finally revealed themselves, which could be literally any moment. Harmonia and the fairies still weren't clear on the evil ones' identities, and all they could do was watch as the evil force conducted a surprise attack on another world, leaving thousands of creatures wounded. I imagined it would be like prepping for an exam, which, sure, I'm comfortable with. Only this time, the exam would be mentally and physically dangerous in a way no normal exam would. So, okay, not really like an exam at all. The mystery of our challenges freaked me out.

But part of me was comforted by Aggro. There had been dozens of Ambassadors before me for thousands of years and from all over the world, with trainers that spoke every language ever spoken. I knew it was no coincidence I had the same trainer as my grandmother.

We made our way into Cantatis, and Aggro met us right at the porthole with a whole scroll of world skills we'd be learning. First on the list: Summoning, an ancient skill every Ambassador and their guide must learn, which involved channeling the powers of the elderly in our time of need.

Most of the elderly, like Wahlil from Lavender Sea, are immortal, but immortality works different in Cantatis than the fairy tales. Each elder is granted immortality after a lifetime of brave acts. Wahlil was a warrior in his day, and was granted immortality and strength on his deathbed by the spirits for living such a selfless life. Wahlil is one of the few that still has his physical body. Many elderly only exist in spirit form and are only visible when an Ambassador is experiencing "true turmoil," Aggro's words, not mine. They know of everything and everyone, and they always hear calls when one of their allies is in danger, but it's how we call them that really makes the difference. That's where the summoning comes in.

"Think of it as a spell," Aggro barked at us. They made everything sound harsh, even if it wasn't.

"A spell? So we really are witches, huh?" Bree quipped.

I hid the beginnings of a smile behind my hand. Of course Bree wasn't intimidated by Aggro. It didn't seem to bother her when they'd smile, and their sharp teeth glinted. I wanted to be like that, unfazed.

"No. Witches use wands. You use your own two hands," They tapped Bree's hand with their paw.

"Have you ever seen your Ambassador markings?" they asked.

I shook my head, confused.

"Here, I show better than I tell."

They had me raise both hands so that my torso stretched with me. What looked like an intricate map lit up on my hands, from my fingers to the inner corners of my elbows.

"These are your markings," Aggro said. "These are maps to all the spirits that can help you. After your first mission, these paths embedded in you and shall be there forever. Only you can see them. You will always have a guide through the realms because of them."

Bree's smirk transformed into awe. I gawked at my arms, feeling stronger by the moment. I felt like if I opened my palms, I'd have enough power to knock down the tree in front of me.

"Together," they instructed, and Bree and I clasped hands.

"Spiritibus dimittam. Spiritibus dimittam. Spiritibus dimittam," they raised their voice, as a soft breeze started up and began to build.

"Repeat! Say it loud!"

Palm to palm, we repeated as loudly as they did, "Spiritibus dimittam! Spiritibus dimittam!"

The more we said it, the stronger the wind grew. The markings on Bree and me were bright and vibrant on our dark skin. I heard voices other than our own. Voices of every tone and timbre, some whispers, some bellows, circling us on the wind. I opened my tightly shut eyes to see the glimmer of all sorts of faces, like hundreds of tints of the same color.

Aggro shouted over the voices, "Focus on the paths written on your body. Think of your breath, your heartbeat. Imagine it all moving at the same time."

We chanted one last time, and without any warning, Aggro broke our hands from each other. Everything stopped.

"Enough."

I held my tongue, I'd been hushed.

Aggro continued, "Any longer, and you would have awoken elders who've been at peace for thousands of years. You must only use this spell as the absolute last resort. The energy it takes to summon the elders is quite draining on the universe. Well done."

It was going to take a lot for me to get used to Aggro's delivery.

They turned their back to us and continued to speak, "I will not be teaching you to fight. If that is what you hoped for, you've met the wrong trainer."

Bree threw up her arms, "Then how are we supposed to win against these creatures? If they're really that bad, won't they just kill us? What are we gonna do, chant at them?"

Bree's words reverberated in my mind. This was the first moment I'd actually considered that this might kill us. We weren't just doing this to protect people from danger, we were working to learn how to keep not just us, but many, alive.

"What sense does it make to end a war by continuing it? Death, plus more death equals death, my child. I'll teach you how to protect yourselves, how to counter attack, yes. But not simply fighting for fighting's sake."

I was dumbfounded.

Apparently, Aggro could tell, "Wars do not end with a never-ending fight. The answer to war is peace, and you two, you can achieve that peace. Now, Bree, since you are a warrior you'll in fact learn a few moves. I will give you a weapon you are to only use in battle. Juniper, you'll learn, well, other strategies."

"How?" I asked.

Aggro turned back around to face us, "Well, that's exactly what I'll be training you for. I'll teach you as much as I can before the first attack. Still, you must be prepared for moments beyond my training."

Confused I asked, "What are those?"

"You shall see." And with that, Aggro vanished before our eyes as they'd do many times in our trainings to come.

We stood side by side in the forest.

"Stay together. Find your way," We heard Aggro's voice echo before the last trace of them went away.

"So what, we have to train ourselves now?"

Bree looked pissed, but I didn't blame her. She found a nice tree to lean on and took a seat. I folded my arms in protest.

After what felt like ten minutes, I decided to take the lead on things, "Why don't we . . . I dunno . . . look around. Learn the space. That's probably what Aggro wants us to do."

Bree hobbled up from the comfortable space she'd made for herself.

"Where you trying to go?" She demanded.

"I don't know. I mean, if Aggro doesn't come back, we at least need to figure out how to get out of here."

She rolled her eyes, "Okay, well, call me when you find a way out."

"Aggro said to stay—"

I stopped myself. I was so annoyed. I didn't feel like trying to convince her to care. I was tired of that being our dynamic.

"Fine."

I wanted to go, so I did. I marched towards the thorny area in the distance, fearful but determined. She lagged behind for a moment before following me.

"Dammit," she mumbled.

I smirked to myself. I totally won that round. I was light on my feet, moving slowly past the vegetation dusted on the ground beneath us. Soon, we had made our way swiftly outside the boundary of trees and deep into a thicket of thorns.

As we slowed to observe our surroundings, something peered out from the tangle of brush. I stopped dead in my tracks. It disappeared, and we took that precious time to duck out of the main path. The thing, whatever it was, raised its gnarly head, then two others joined it, as if choreographed. I thought it couldn't see us behind the giant bushel of green we'd found, but then it looked directly at me.

The things began to prowl toward us, moving eerily slow. They were small goblin-like creatures with prickly, hairy bodies.

"We have to get out of here!" Bree whispered, so loud she might as well have screamed.

I grabbed Bree's arm, turning her to face me, "This is exactly what Aggro told us not to do. We can't panic. We have to stay calm."

The day before we began training, Aggro kept telling us, "The key to failure is fear."

They said it so much I was playing it over in my head at that very moment. I replayed their words like a song.

We backed away slowly at first, the little ghouls moving at our pace. I attempted to hide my fear as I sped up slowly.

I grabbed Bree's arm, "Okay, on three, let's turn and run."

She nodded.

"One. Two. Three! "

As we gained speed something grabbed onto my ankle and I went down like a sack of bricks. I looked down at my foot, which was caught in the grip of an enchanted vine with long, stinging spines. Tears sprang to my eyes, as I tried to break away.

"Bree!" I shrieked at Bree who'd kept running ahead.

She stopped and scrambled back to me. She tried her hardest to rip the weed from my leg, but it was impossible. I glanced behind us. They moved slow, but the creatures were much closer than I'd expected. She began to rip harder at the weed, but it stayed in place, and my leg was getting bloodier by the second.

When they were close enough, one of the creatures shouted, "What do you do on our marsh?"

I made out an "X" scar on its spiky forehead. Words failed me. My throat was way too dry. We were helpless and increasingly frantic. Body paralyzed by terror, I tried to formulate a plan. We needed something, anything, but I had nothing.

"We don't want anything from you! We're not your enemy!"

One of the goblins tsked, "Humans."

Another turned its attention to me, "We like humans!"

"Nice and gamey!" Another one sneered.

One especially coarse goblin touched my leg, trailing the weed trap with its tail, unfazed by the thorns. I kicked reflexively and in vain.

It laughed.

Its sticky, putrid paws wrapped around my arm.

"Let's try some raw!" one suggested.

They all turned to their companion with his paw on my arm. It pinched the widest part of my bicep, its claws already drawing blood. There was no doubt in my mind they would have killed us. The pain crowded my head and flowed out of me in a scream so loud that Earthlings might have heard it.

Suddenly, it released me. At first, I struggled to understand why. I was confused, my breath ragged. The goblins stared past me.

Bree circled around me and squeezed me like we were best friends.

Her eyes widened and I noticed my leg was freed from the trap. I turned my head to find Aggro standing there. They stomped three times, and everything went black. We traveled through space and stars so fast that Bree looked like a blur beside me. Within seconds, the vortex greedily pulled us out into a totally unfamiliar public bathroom.

Aggro spoke, but we couldn't see them, "Stand. Explore."

I grabbed the bathroom sink, expecting to feel pain when I stood, but nothing. I looked down at normal brown skin: no red, no cuts or bruises. I stared in the mirror at Bree behind me. Her face said, *Where are we?* But no words came out. I shrugged.

A tall blonde man barged in and without a second passing muttered, "Sorry! So sorry. Excuse me," before backing out.

Bree led us out, and the same guy gawked at us and made his way back into the bathroom. We turned a corner into a large room full of books upon books, stacked higher than some of the tallest buildings in Evershire, all surrounding several long benches. A few folks read quietly to themselves.

"Follow my voice," a voice like gravel barked.

"Aggro?"

Bree turned her head, and I looked in front of us: no sign of Aggro at all. But still, we hurried to the entryway where the voice seemed closest. Right outside of it was an open space leading to a sidewalk full of strangers. We paused.

"Keep moving."

We obeyed invisible Aggro into a sea of pedestrians, all with arguably better understandings of where they were going than we had. The street was cobblestone, and the buildings were the old sort of greyish brick I'd only ever seen online. If it weren't for the Nikes and yoga pants crossing our path every second, I might have thought we'd gone back in time.

A bright red, double-decker bus rolled into view.

A tour guide spoke from a microphone, "The nursery rhyme '*London Bridge*,' known and recited all over the world in various versions, came into being when—"

I couldn't make out the last of her words as the bus drove out of sight, but I didn't need to.

Bree gasped, "We're in London!"

For a moment, we just lingered there in the middle of the sidewalk. My feet planted on cobblestone, as people shoved past us on their commutes to who knows where. Thoughts swirled in my head and turned into nonsense as I tried to take in the crowd while still finding my footing.

"Turn to your right," Aggro instructed.

I jumped.

Aggro led us into a cluttered alley that smelled like urine and beer. Grimy walls were covered with street art, and each step was either sticky or met with some sort of trash. An older man with a scruffy grey beard moved towards us, and I'd be playing if I said my heart didn't skip a beat with the fear of a thousand cowards.

"Good afternoon, ladies," he smirked, pausing too close to us.

Bree sucked her teeth. I nudged her, afraid any sort of response would make him react. I wouldn't even look him in the eye.

"You don't talk?" He asked with a gritty English accent.

"You don't take hints?" Bree stood strong with her arms folded, staring right at this guy like he wasn't a creep who could literally kill us.

Throwing his hands up first to make one last remark, "Eh, alright! Just trying to spread some cheer. Good riddance." He finally walked away.

I only had courage to speak when he was totally out of sight.

"What the hell is wrong with you?" I felt like my mom scolding her.

"We have to placate him, why?"

"Cause he could have literally killed us if we didn't."

"Well, if he was really trying to kill us, I don't see how us saying what's up really would have stopped him."

I didn't know what to say. I couldn't predict what would have happened; I was just glad nothing did. We were quiet for a moment in that unbearable alley.

Aggro made themselves known once more, "Find the child's face. That will be your exit."

Their voice echoed in the alley, like some sort of god. *The child's face.* There were no children anywhere near us. The walls, though, were full of portraits. A feminine silhouette with hair covering its face, a dragon painted orange and white, but no child. Bree tapped my shoulder. I followed her finger.

"A child's face."

Sure enough, there was a portrait of a girl with a short bob smiling at passersby. Her green eyes pierced into me as if she were real. They glowed, even. No, they literally glowed, into a bright green, then yellow, as a light around the figure became a circle, which became a vortex. Bree and I were sucked in.

A sudden glitch in my vision broke my focus. A forceful pressure plunged us towards the ground. Bree latched onto me, and we pulled each other close. We landed, barely missing the knotty roots of a larger-than-life tree. The ground beneath us was veiled in murky fog.

"You're safe now," Aggro rumbled.

The fog around them faded, revealing their unsettling face, but still I was comforted.

"You were in more danger than you may have realized," Harmonia drifted out of the fog, revealing herself.

"Why did you send us to London of all places?" I demanded.

"That, I didn't do. Someone, something, interfered with the channels."

The whole time, I'd assumed Aggro was in charge. I retroactively lost my balance. Chills broke out on my body.

"What do you mean, 'something'?"

Bree was bold. She stood tall and angry like commanding attention without needing to say anything more.

"We don't know," Aggro looked away uncharastically weary.

"How do you not know? You're supposed to be our trainer. If you don't know, then does anyone?" My anger bolstered my fear.

What have I gotten myself into? I thought.

Harmonia commanded our attention, "Listen to me. We've deduced that the 'something' interfering with the channel must be shape-shifters. That narrows things down to just a handful of creatures. Something that can use the portholes, like you, and can do something I cannot—travel to other planets with you both, inconspicuously."

"So you're saying whatever took us into London was there with us, *looking* like us?" Bree scowled.

She scowled, rolled her eyes and squinted through a glare emitting just how pissed she was.

"They must be the Mutabo. It seems this war we've been waiting for has indeed made its way to Earth. Unfortunately, we did not prepare for things to escalate this quickly."

Harmonia usually pristine, round face was veiled in discomfort.

I was over the edge, I was falling from a cliff without a ledge to grab onto. While I fell into oblivion, Bree held her ground.

"We're not even trained yet. How are we going to help you if we can't fight with you?"

"You're correct, there's so little time. But as I've said before, and will repeat as much as necessary, I am not here to teach you to fight."

Aggro held their head high, but kept their eyes on me and Bree. I was growing increasingly tired of the whole "we don't fight" talk. I imagined all the potentially sketchy people we encountered in London. Any one of them could have been one of those creatures, ready to kill us.

As if reading my mind, Harmonia said, "I understand your fear. No one has control over everything and everyone. Whoever is causing trouble is masterful at it. This is all I will say now. The channels should be safe to travel for the moment, but not for long. Our elders are growing weaker by the day as the Mutabo have meddled with so many worlds already. You will go back to Earth now. Return tomorrow, and we'll begin your intensive war training. Do you understand?"

We nodded.

"Now, both of you must go. At once."

CHAPTER NINE

Dad and Auntie had reached the intensive research part of their study, which meant long hours in the lab and fewer site trips with Bree and me. I didn't mind it so much, since they were paying Robbie Jr. to pick up the slack of not having a second person to help. But I didn't like that I never got to see my dad. When our paths did cross, sometimes at dinner or early in the morning, he looked like a zombie. He'd never admit it, but I could tell he and Auntie weren't getting along. At dinner one night, Uncle Robbie asked how things were going in the lab.

"Well, they would be fine if we were more thorough about a few things," Auntie said, condescendingly.

My dad said nothing back, choosing instead to begrudgingly stuff his face with pasta. Nope, he just scarfed down macaroni like it was his last meal.

Finally, he looked up and noticed we were all staring and laughed, "I'd say things are going pretty well actually."

I watched his smile fade. I felt a tinge of secondhand embarrassment for him. The awkwardness in the room was thick, and the look on Auntie's face was fierce. I'd only ever known her to be kind and reassuring; she was only precise and sterile when she needed to be, in the lab. Even though I missed it, I didn't even care if me and Bree could go to the site anymore. I just wanted them to hurry up and makes some strides on their research, so they could get back to being friendly.

I overheard Dad and Auntie arguing the night before. I didn't catch the whole conversation, but it sounded like Auntie was against releasing their new information about the Valeferus to their scientist colleagues like they'd originally planned. This was confusing to me, since dad explained early on the need to keep his university abreast of their finding.

My dad always used to say, "There's no need to argue science," but I guess this part of it wasn't what he was talking about. Maybe it's because they had to actually see each other everyday. Maybe they had different working styles or communication skills. All I knew for sure was I'd never seen them hate each other so much.

On break days when they wouldn't go to the lab, my dad would act like everything was chill. He would write in his lab folder for hours in the living room.

Mom asked him how the work was going, and he'd say, "Brilliantly. I'm very excited."

But then the day would end, and he'd huddle back into the forbidden lab with this new, grumpy Auntie Elaine. She was constantly angry about something, even on days off. Uncle called her out on it after she gave him the "talk to the hand" when he asked her a question.

"Well, somebody's grumpy today!" He said half joking, but I know he wasn't joking.

Finally, one sunny morning, Dad summoned us to help them again.

"We've got a lot to do, so I suggest you wear your worst clothes!" He shouted as he came up the stairs of the basement. "Here we go."

Cue Bree's signature eye roll. I was at the point in our relationship that I just expected her to roll her eyes at things. I didn't even mind it; it was like tapping legs while sitting or sucking teeth, just a reflex, I guess, only cheekier.

Dad wasn't kidding about that day being a busy one. Never mind the fact I was also preoccupied with like, I don't know, saving the world. We were supposed to meet with Aggro before sunset, and from what my dad was saying, I really worried that wouldn't even happen.

"After today, we've got just two more drives up. Then it's all lab. So, we've got some serious wrapping up to do. Serious."

Hearing him talk about finishing the project, at least the site part, made me proud. I unpacked four shovels at the bottom of the trunk. Auntie started barking orders before I could hand them out.

"Start digging where you see that flag," she instructed.

She sounded curt against my dad's enthusiasm. How my dad could stay upbeat around her baffled me. I looked around until I spotted the flag next to the start of a small crater. Every part of the worksite was level, except for this hole, only a few inches deep.

Bree and I walked over and began to dig while Dad picked up a shovel and began on the opposite side.

"Perfect, Bree, now just keep it up. We're hoping to hit the jackpot here."

My dad loves to be the motivator. He's like a marathon coach, always giving more encouragement the harder things get. I love him for that.

As he helped us dig, he began raving about their findings so far, "Remember that hunch I had?"

He didn't wait for us to answer, "This is it. From the studies we've done so far, I strongly believe, there is a chance that this Valeferus is not just a plant, but a vegetable. It's possible that we came to this site right after the fruit of the plant ripened; and even more possible that it fell from the plant before we had the chance to see it. We just haven't been able to find proof yet." His eyes glimmered.

"June, I don't see you digging," Auntie chided from the other side of camp.

She was right, I wasn't digging, but neither was she. Instead, she shuffled through some papers by the van.

Dad let out a short laugh and cleared his throat. I was digging mindlessly when suddenly I wedged the spade into the ground, and I couldn't pull it out again.

Out of nowhere, gusts of wind blew my curls into the air and my ass onto the ground. It wasn't a windy day, no chance of rain. I was dumbfounded.

Dad's eyes flashed wildly around, before he shouted back at us, "To the trees! C'mon!"

He ran to the biggest tree, wrapped one arm around the trunk as much as he could, and held the other out to us.

"Hurry!"

Every step took tremendous effort. The wind was so strong it created a small tornado made of debris and papers.

I got to the tree, and Dad pulled me in, Bree rushing over behind us. I closed my eyes to wait until the wind calmed. All of a sudden, everything went still. I opened my eyes to find everything that was falling just froze into place. My heart pounded as I let go of the branch. Bree followed suit, but my dad had held tight, still frozen. I was entranced by his stillness, his face stuck in a panic.

I was too displaced to respond the first time Bree shouted, "Where is my mom!"

As if on cue, a smoke-like figure carried Auntie's limp body out of the woods.

Bree in utter dismay yelled, "Mom! Ma! What did you do to her?"

The figure walked to the middle of the clearing, easily pushing past suspended litter, and dropped Auntie, though she only fell halfway before floating right above the ground. I backed away in horror, my eyes locked on this ominous dark, blue figure, even though this instinctive fear in the pit of my stomach made me want to veer away. Instead of feet it had dark clouds that left remnants of themselves wherever they crossed. I followed its movements as it bent over Auntie Elaine. Right in front of me, the form dissipated and fused into her. It *became* her. Auntie's once-limp body anchored upright, and she stood up.

"What the fuck is happening?" Bree whimpered.

She frowned across from me, her hands on her head, yelling something that my fear muted. Auntie's possessed body sauntered towards a portal that had begun to open in front of us. Through trash and fog, I saw Aggro appear through the portal from the inside. They moved closer to the entrance into our world but did not cross. Instead the bellowed from the other side,

"Spiritibus dimittam! Spiritibus dimittam! Leave!"

Their voice reverberating over the forest around us. With that, the strange ghostly figure seeped out of Auntie's body and evaporated into thin air. Auntie collapsed to the ground. Bree ran over to her mom and shook her unconscious body.

"Come, we must go," Aggro ordered still inside the portal.

I pulled at Bree, but she wouldn't move, "What about them? Are we supposed to just leave my mom here?"

She crouched in the dirt with Auntie's head in her lap. I had questions too, ones to which I wasn't sure I wanted the answers.

"They're safe now. No time for questions. Come," Aggro told us.

Bree placed her mom's head softly on the ground and gave me a look I hope to never see again. We moved somberly to the porthole. I gave in to the magnet force of the vortex. I knew nothing, I felt everything.

We fell into mud, surrounded by fairies wielding bows and arrows. I ducked, as a stone wrapped in flames hurled over the deep ditch we were trapped in.

The fairy homes above us fell to the ground, their inhabitants fluttering around in panic. We were in the midst of a heated battle. Strange creatures, like vicious oxen standing on hind legs, lurched towards us. Aggro hopped out of the ditch and threw a rope down for us.

"Move! The Mutabo are fierce!" Aggro ordered before handing Bree a knife, nodding towards the beach not too far in front of us.

But what would usually be a simple stroll felt like a ten-mile trek. There were dozens of creatures who looked like Aggro fighting the Mutabo. Fairies with shields floated high in the trees around them, throwing down what looked like rocks, only when they hit a creature, they would leave the Mutabo out of commission for moments at a time, as if temporarily paralyzed. Bree swung her knife at air more to intimidate than actually fight.

Aggro fended off one of the Mutabo that stood especially taller than the rest. Another swung its fist at me and I ran like I had an "X" on my back.

Bree shouted to me, "Wait!"

I crouched behind robust tree surrounded by shrubbery and waited for Bree to catch up. A fire ball hissed past my head. She squatted next to me and handed me a sword she must have found. I only knew a few moves from training and grew nervous just thinking how I'd execute them.

"Let's do it then!" She charged towards the Mutabo swinging fearlessly.

Aggro leapt and helped fend off the giant Mutabo, who almost stabbed Bree right in the chest.

"Don't let them scare you!" Aggro warned.

A Mutabo knocked Bree to the ground. While she was down, she kicked it forcefully enough to make it lose balance, then she scrambled up and sliced it right in the arm. I held my sword in front of me like a shield, but hadn't yet tried to use it. A Mutabo roared towards me from behind and I ducked, just missing it. I drew my sword and yelled threats to the air, but the large Mutabo only laughed. It bore its fist into my stomach and I was thrust to the ground. The wind was literally knocked out of me. In slow motion I witnessed the creature ready to punch me again. Surely this would be my undoing. That is, if Bree hadn't come in and sliced the Mutabo from the belly up. It doubled over and held its stomach. She sliced at its legs on at a time. Finally that Mutabo retreated, but others were close behind.

"Run!" Bree commanded, and so I did as soon as I caught my breath again. She jumped up to her feet and let out a war cry, "Ahhh!"

I looked back to see Bree stab another Mutabo. When I'd turned straight ahead again, I saw Mutabo in front of me I hadn't seen before. They were closing in on me.

"Bree!" I yelled back, but they were closing in on her too.

I held my sword out as six large Mutabo encircled me. There's no way I could fight them all, I wasn't even sure I could defeat one. I was losing hope. I could see Bree, trapped, through the openings between Mutabo.
One Mutabo, wearing a steel plate on its chest, stepped in closer to me, "Where do ye think you're going?"

"You better go, or I swear we'll kill you." I hoped it wouldn't call my bluff.

I pointed my sword at its face. I imagined a me that could end that Mutabo's life without a second thought, for even considering to try me. I imagined the beach where Aggro had instructed us to go. The elders power was so strong there Mutabo didn't dare go. But it wasn't close enough for me. I could feel the ocean breeze from where I stood. I wanted to be there more than anything.

"There are too many! We have to call the elders," Bree shouted.

My Ambassador markings began to glow. Aggro and their army stormed into view, striking down each Mutabo within seconds of the next.

"Whoa," Bree and I whispered at the same time.

Aggro circled us, "This battle has been won by the Mutabo. The mass have them have retreated to their quarters with many of our people as prisoner. I am sorry to say, many of us have died. This is not over."

How will we win next time when we've failed so badly?

I slumped, overwhelmed. I felt like I'd fallen in the deep end before I'd learned to swim. Aggro passed a paw over Bree's small wounds, murmuring something over and over. Bree watched in awe as the blood from her side and shoulder disappeared.

"Listen now. The smoky creature that tried to overtake your mother today was indeed a Mutabo. And Bree, I must tell you that your mother is now a part of this, too."

Bree herself off, "What the hell do you mean my mother? She has nothing to do with this, y'all said so yourselves."

Aggro didn't look like they wanted to say, but they did anyway, "These creatures are able to take over human bodies and make them their own for a short time. A Mutabo has been using your mother as a host."

"What?"

Bree's expression was angry and confused. It's like she'd heard the words but didn't know how to categorize them. I watched her thinking, brewing.

"How long has she been like this?" I asked, remembering how strange Auntie had been lately.

Aggro spoke in a low, deliberate tone, "I cannot say for sure. They are able to inhabit humans for only hours at a time. I do know that it did not mean to expose itself earlier. The Mutabo are growing weaker as their mainland is deteriorating. This will be to our advantage."

"What do these things want my mom for, anyway?" Bree held back tears.

"I apologize, I do not know. Mutabo are powerful and intelligent, and there are many reasons they could have chosen to inhabit your mother. But you will find out. That will be your focus now."

"How the hell do we stop them? We don't even have that much training! Oh, wait, you don't know, right?" Tears slowly flowed down Bree's face. She wiped them bitterly.

"Bree, we're going to make sure your mom's okay. We're gonna figure this out," I really, really hoped what I said would be true.

But I knew just as little about how we could fix all this. I was still drowning in that pool of doubt I'd found myself in a while ago. Still, I let myself believe.

Aggro continued, "Mutabo transfer worlds every thousand years, and that time has come again. We believe that since they've taken over your mother, they must be looking to Earth to be their next target. That is why I had you take part in this battle today. This was the first. Mutabo are here to kill Earthly allies to make this mission easier for them. The war has surely begun."

Every breath was a strain. I used to ask myself what Grandma would do in tough situations, but in that moment, I couldn't even imagine. When I was really little, I'd cook up fantastical stories of how she'd fix things if she were me. If Grandma was me, she'd win a science fair with a new invention and get to meet the president because of it; if she was me, she'd be able to talk herself out of trouble after getting caught sneaking Skittles in middle school. She was clever, bold, innovative. But no matter how hard I tried, I just couldn't imagine what she'd do in this moment. This was far beyond any problem I could have ever envisioned before Cantatis became a part of my life.

Aggro softly rested their sword in its holster, "Juniper, it's time you develop your teleporting skills. The increased dangers to both our worlds require it. For now, stay close to your town. Jump from street to street, corner to corner. I will tell you when you may jump countries. And a strong word of advice: stay together."

Stay together. I was getting so tired of hearing that.

With that, he sent us down a rather rocky portal back to our site. Everything fell from midair, and time resumed, but I still held my breath until I saw my dad's breath continue naturally again.

"Are you alright?" He asked me.

I nodded. He had no idea. Bree ran to her mom's side.

Auntie rose slowly from the ground, chuckled and coughed, "That was something."

I was happy to see her okay, but a big part of me feared it wasn't even her.

Dad furrowed his brow and rubbed his forehead, "How 'bout we all call it a day?"
He laughed his throaty laugh, and I laughed too, hoping I sounded casual.

Chapter Ten

The scent of fresh cilantro and cumin floated into the living room. I sat on a plush recliner in the family room, a cozy space I hadn't taken advantage of before. It was rainy and slow, a "board game day," as Grandma would call it. It seemed peaceful on the outside, but I knew it was simply the calm before the storm. I was trying to relaxed, but inside, my mind was racing. I wanted to know, needed to know, when Auntie was herself and when she was a Mutabo. I replayed every encounter I'd had with her over the past few days. Moments when I thought she was excessively irritable or strange, moments when she was quiet when normally she'd be talking. And that day, a normal day for most people. Was she Auntie, then? I watched her like a hawk.

Bree and I agreed to practice teleporting that night. We were going to meet Sen and Vera on the beach, but instead of walking halfway and trying to catch a cab once we made it to civilization, I'd have to get us there with magic. Easy.

Meeting with Sen was my idea. Ever since meeting her, I'd wanted to see her again. I was preoccupied with saving the world, but I couldn't wait to pounce on my first opportunity to see her again. I could barely believe she really existed. Just the thought of her voice made me feel like I was floating; the thought of kissing her made me melt. I kept replaying her smile when our eyes first met in my mind.

So to say I was excited about that night would be an understatement. Bree and I figured the best time would be after dinner, when everyone quieted down. But even at this hour, it was anything but calm in the McKinney house.

Robbie Jr. held one hand over Bree's head as she attempted to read. The McKinneys had no TV, which encouraged everyone to use the sizeable bookshelf, accented with books like Barack Obama's memoir, *Dreams of My Father*. On this particular day, Bree was reading a copy of *Raisin in the Sun*.

"I'm not even touching you," Junior taunted.

She swatted at him and whispered-shouted, "Stop! You play too much. Damn!"

Somehow, some way, Uncle Robbie heard her and hollered back, "Bree!"

She set her jaw and slumped in the recliner.

"Anybody fighting gets no pie. You been warned!"

Junior withdrew his finger and bounced, trying to pretend he'd been minding his business the whole time. This boy was nothing if not driven by bribes. I heard Auntie and Dad arguing from the lab room stairs.

"Hey," I tapped Bree.

She shrugged me away, but I had no time to get annoyed. I crept to the hallway. I wanted to hear every little thing they had to say.

"We have two weeks," Auntie warned. "We've got to move more quickly than this if we're going finalize this formula any time soon."

Her voice was gruff and short, Dad was reassuring. He told her they were on track and would only be a couple days off at most.

She wasn't having it, "No finished product, no success,"

Dad didn't respond. They went their separate ways. I turned to creep back in the living room and jumped after discovering Bree was right behind me the whole time.

"So what do we do?" she asked me.

Like I had any idea. I caught my breath and thought for a moment.

"How about we test her? Or it. Like, how about we ask it a bunch of questions at dinner? If it's still here, we might get some answers. Maybe make the Mutabo stumble a little."

She nodded. I have no idea what athletes feel like before a big game, but I'd imagine it was something like how I felt before dinner that night. I tried to let myself get lost in the savory broth wafting in the air, reminding me of holidays with Grandma. I made my way to my seat at the kitchen table. Uncle placed a large pot of stew in the middle of everyone.

"Mmm," Robbie rubbed his hands together like a scheming cartoon character.

"What's that?" I asked.

Uncle Robbie pointed to the pot, "This here is chicken stew. Over there is some mashed potatoes, carrots, and some rolls I baked up this morning."

He looked pleased with all he'd made. Robbie scooped out a serving of the mashed potatoes for himself and slopped it right in the middle of his plate. He made his way towards the living room, but Uncle stopped him dead in his tracks.

"Oh no, you don't." He pointed to a chair next to me, and Robbie sat, the very picture of innocence.

"Not often we all get to be at the table, all of us together," Uncle's smile was especially big, because Auntie (or a Mutabo) had just entered the room. "How's the lab work?"

"Well, there's been a bit of a setback." Dad started, but Auntie cut him off, "No setback. We just need to move quicker." She pushed her food around with a fork, "Much quicker."

I nudged Bree. She noisily slurped her soup.

"So, Ma, how're you feeling about everything since you're almost done? That's like super exciting, right?"

There was a slight pause, but not an incriminating one, before she answered, "Excited? Excitement is not key; serum is key. That's what I would call 'exciting.'"

Auntie continued to eat as if what she said wasn't ominous and strange. I glanced at Bree to find her looking back at me, with what I felt was probably my same expression. Discomfort. Other than chewing and the occasional loud breath, the table was quiet.

Dad chimed in, "I for one am mighty excited. This is years in the making and just moments from completion. It's a phenomenal thing."

Everyone nodded and made sounds of polite agreement and then the room grew quiet again. We just couldn't shake the strange aura Auntie was emitting. I mulled over what to say. How to move this awkward conversation forward. The serum was so important to this Mutabo, that I knew. But I had no idea why. So I asked a silly question — silly because Dad talked about the answer far too often for me not to know.

"What's the serum?" I inquired with my best naive expression.

Dad opened his mouth to speak, but Auntie beat him to it, "It's the sum of all our parts. Once we have a serum, we'll be commissioned to start trials on humans. "

"What if you don't have the serum by the 'deadline'. Isn't there a set deadline?" I pushed.

"We will have the serum by deadline!" The Mutabo barked.

My neck got warm. I started to itch. Bree must have been thinking what I was thinking, because she'd put her spoon down and shot me a look.

"Elaine, come on now!" Uncle scrunched his napkin.

His shoulders were tight, and so was his face. Mutabo Auntie took a deep breath. Her grin relaxed into a smirk I think she meant to be calming. But I'm telling you, it was not calming.

And then she said, "I mean, of course it will be ready. We were to have it days ago, but that's fine. Just fine."

Her lips stretched thin to mimic a smile.

"I'm sure it's hard working day in, day out on such a big project." Mom peeped, chuckling awkwardly.

Uncle got up, "E, you wanna come help me with something?"

He headed to the hallway, still glaring. The Mutabo followed.

"Well! Somebody needs her nap." Bree quipped.

The Mutabo glared back at Bree, and for a second, I was scared it would attack.

Dad, the king of giving people the benefit of the doubt, was still trying to cape for this . . . thing, "We've both been stressed. Even I wanted to pull my hair out this morning."

It made me sad for him. He had no idea what he was dealing with.

"She probably just needs to rest," Mom added.

It was clear everyone was doing their own version of damage control. It's moments like those I would have loved to yell to the rooftops about Cantatis. I hated this monster making Auntie seem so horrible, and her having no say in the matter. Feeling helpless and in need of recharging I asked,

"Can I go?"

I needed space. I needed to think, to plan. Mom nodded, and I hopped up placing my plate in the sink. I beckoned to Bree to come upstairs with me.

"We have to keep checking in with them to find out when this serum thing is ready," she said as soon as the bedroom door closed.

I agreed, "We can't let them get hold of it. It's got to have something to do with the Mutabo's master plan."

Now we had to figure out *how* to get hold of the serum. Especially since Dad had told me numerous times the lab was off limits.

We had just a little time before we'd planned to meet with Sen and Vera at the beach. We'd have to put the Mutabo investigation on hold. My energy funneled into the night. I went to wash-up, hoping I'd wash away my stress along with it. I studied the freshly-washed baby face staring back at me.

"Hmm." I murmured out loud without meaning to. I'd never looked at myself so closely. My eyes followed my face from my baby hair down to my thick eyebrows, big dark eyes, my lips with the exaggerated cupid's bow I inherited from my mom and Grandma. I felt older than the young face staring back at me. But I also still felt young, very, very young. I had a strong sense of desire to play with my look. I wanted to look as bold as I felt. Bree came into the bathroom and sprayed her short hair with water. She then applied mascara and said,

"Here," And handed it to me. I'm not sure how she knew that was just what I needed.

"Thanks," I said as I grabbed the mascara and put some on the tops and bottoms of my curly eyelashes. My eyes grew even bigger and I looked more awake. I know mascara is nothing for some people, but for me it was like a boost, a B12 vitamin in a makeup stick. I fluffed my curls and smiled. I changed into one of my only shirts without words on it, a dark blue short-sleeve crew neck.

We finally went downstairs to find an empty kitchen. Everyone had dispersed. Mom read quietly in the living room. Aunt Elaine was combing Marci's hair in the loveseat like her old self. I really hoped it was her. It was finally quiet enough. It was time.

We tiptoed out the back door and scurried to the garden in pitch-black darkness, with only the light from Bree's phone that she'd snuck out of her mom's bag leading the way. The portal beside the fountain opened, and I closed my eyes, picturing that old, rundown building where Bree would hang out. Bree took my hand, and we were drawn in.

My eyes were shut. It was the only way I could focus without freaking out. A thrust of power plunged us to the dusty ground beside a tin trash can. Next to us was the entry to that basement I'd climbed down almost a month ago. I dusted myself off and caught my balance.

A dark figure edged over from the front of the building. I immediately lost any of that balance I'd just found.

"Bree? June?"

The silhouette came closer, and the street light illuminated Sen. My cheeks got hot. I itched from my neck down, and my throat was so dry I felt like I'd done a cinnamon challenge. Vera wasn't far behind her but I couldn't keep my eyes off Sen.

"Um, yeah?" I clicked my heels together, trying to put my body at attention.

Sen's warm smile made me feel more human and even more nervous. I shoved my shaky hands in my pockets. It was chilly for a summer night, but I couldn't tell if my shivers were from the cold or my nerves.

"Did you come the long way?" Vera asked Bree.

She shrugged and looked to me. I shrugged back and smiled to myself. *Oh no, actually we got here via vortex.* I must have been too in my own head, because Bree slapping me on the shoulder is the last thing I remember.

"Yep, we had to leave extra early just to get here on time. Right, June?"

I nodded slowly, still on another plane, still stuck on our unusual transportation. Or the whole reason we used a vortex in the first place. I tried to focus. I needed to be present. I needed to not think about Cantatis for just a moment. Bree waltzed off ahead of me to Vera, oozing with mischief.

"So, the beach is, like, ten more minutes that way," Vera pointed straight ahead.

The breeze from the ocean got stronger with each step. Sen kept a leisurely pace. She had this slow kind of walk that only confident people can pull off. The kind that doesn't seem phased by how quickly or slowly the people around her are moving. I slowed my frantic steps to meet hers. We were all silent, and the silence started to feel too loud so I decided to break the ice.

"So, you and Bree are . . . good friends?" Inside I was cringing but I didn't let Sen see. I really wish I was better at talking. I rarely initiate conversations though, so I had that in my favor, or so I hoped. I wasn't sure and so I told myself to just be natural, whatever that is. And then I realized I didn't know what that looked like. Isn't it weird how when you tell yourself to be natural it gets even harder to do?

"Ah, yeah. She was the first person I met when I moved here."

"Where did you move from?" I was struggling to find something to say.

"Hawaii. My dad's job transferred him here."

"Do you miss it, Hawaii?" I asked.

"Yeah, I mean it's beautiful there. And the culture's different I guess."

I nodded, returning to my initial plan to "act natural". I must have been doing it wrong because Sen asked,

"You ok?"

I realized I'd been playing with the lone curl I tend to grab when I'm not sure what else to do. I hoped I didn't look nervous.

I dropped the curl and said, "Oh, yeah. Definitely."
I focused on my breath to make sure I was breathing at all. This whole "natural" thing wasn't working out for me. I stuffed my hands in my pockets and breathed again.

"I'm just a little cold." I added.

"You want my jacket?" She took it off before I could respond and draped it over my shoulders.

I'm really not one to give two shits about fake romance in the movies, but I loved that she gave me her windbreaker. I rolled my eyes and laughed. I mean, I couldn't help it. Sen started laughing too, until we were both giggling about giggling.

I looked up at Sen and said, "Thank you."

I ran my hands over the nylon of her jacket. I liked how the breeze made it billow over my shoulders.

She looked down at me and smiled, "Yeah, of course."

In front of us, Vera took a long drag of her cigarette and loudly said to Bree,

"Girl is so *sprung*," and started cracking up.

"She likes her, you think?"

I couldn't tell if Bree was feigning ignorance or not. I was glad she didn't agree with Vera and make this whole thing that much more awkward.

"Is Vera always so..." I was going to say "extra".

"Obnoxious? Yes," Sen finished.

We both laughed. I started to hear the ocean breeze more, and I could finally see the beautiful, dark abyss of the sea. We made it to some steps that led to the sandy beach. I started to untie my shoes.

"So, no New York accent, huh?" she said with a hoity toity New Yawker impression.

I pulled off my right shoe, "What?"

"Aren't you from New York?"

I laughed, "I wish! I mean, yeah, I'm from the north. But not Not New York City. I've always wanted to live there though. I love the chaos of it."

"I could see you living there. I feel like you'd fit right in."

I blushed. I swooned. She *saw* me.

Sen sat next to me and pulled off her loosely tied Converse, "People always say I have an accent. My parents speak fluent Japanese. I mean I do, too, but like . . . I dunno, I wanna tell people like, 'Yeah, I have an accent, and so do you. We all do!'"

I laughed.

"You're right. I never thought of it that way," I said through giggles.

Her hand touched mine. I played it cool. Or at least my version of that. Listening to her talk helped get my mind off how nervous it made me to sit next to her. We were quiet for a moment watching Bree and Vera laugh together while smoking in front of us.

"You wanna know something wild? I fell off a cliff into an ocean once." Sen said, continuing our banter.

"Why, how . . . Why did you . . . How?" I laughed. Then realizing it may not have meant to be funny I backpedaled,

"I mean, I'm sorry if something terrible happened. It's not funny! I just…"

"No! It's okay. I was like eleven. Playing swords with a friend of mine, like some Dungeons & Dragons-type game. We were playing off a boulder at the beach, which in hindsight was a horrible idea. He swung the sword around and knocked me in the water! I freaked the fuck out, but thankfully I didn't hit any rocks or anything. I swam to shore, and everything was fine, but man, I'll never forget it. It was like in slow motion."

Sen threw her head back and let out the most endearing, throaty laugh. I replayed her story in my head, comparing it to my battle training in Cantatis. A few month ago I never would have been able to relate but it felt good that I could then. Still, I wanted to be adventurous beyond Cantatis. I admired Sen's natural daredevil inclination.

"How 'bout you?" Sen had eased down from laughing, and her eyes were set right on mine.

"What?" I worried I'd missed something.

"I mean, like, have you ever gotten yourself into some crazy shit for no reason? You got any wild stories?"

"No! Nothing like that," I felt like such a lie but as far as she was concerned it was true. I was upset I couldn't just tell her all I'd been doing, how I was adventurous too sometimes. All she could ever know was straight-edged, goody-two-shoes June.

"Guess you play it pretty safe, huh?"

She was joking, but since I was already thinking that, it only made me feel more wack.
I tried some sarcasm, my go-to when saying things I wish were true, but definitely aren't, "Me? Safe? Never."

I coughed, hoping it sounded halfway like a laugh. I wished I could tell her about all that had happened since I arrived in Evershire. I wanted her to think I was a spontaneous babe.

"What's the craziest thing you've ever done?", she asked, reminding me of my very plain reality outside of Cantatis.

I toyed with joking about the other worlds without revealing anything important, but I was afraid I'd fumble and say too much. Afraid I'd put my foot in my mouth for the sake of impressing someone. It wasn't worth it, even for Sen.

"First, you tell me how you got this tattoo."

I pointed to a small moon on the inside of her forearm. She leaned over, and I grazed it by mistake, but she didn't seem to mind.

She began trailing it with her fingers, "I did it myself—"

"You lovebirds gonna make out or what?" Vera shouted from the post she and Bree had been leaning on.

I shifted away from Sen like I'd just learned she had cooties. She put her hand on mine, and I looked up at those brown eyes. Bree ran towards us barefoot.

"Wanna swim?" she asked, gesturing towards the ocean.

Sen stood and waited for me to grab my shoes. She grabbed my hand, and we ran to shore.

"Woo!" Bree jumped on my back and knocked me off balance.

I teetered a few steps before shouting, "Bree!"

Vera pumped her fist in the air and started chanting, *Go swim, go swim,* which Bree joined in on.

My toes grazed the edges of the water. In a moment of daring, I threw off my t-shirt and shorts and lunged into the darkness in just my underwear. Letting the waves pull me forward. This was my chance to create one of those "wild" stories Sen asked me about and I wanted that with every fiber of my being. And what better place to do that than in the water, the ocean — my second home.

That night was the first time I felt like I'd started a bold journey. I know, I know, I'd technically already started saving the world and what not, but that night was totally up to me and my desires. I jumped in the ocean because my heart told me to.

"June!" Bree called out.

I heard her laughing as she chased after me. I drifted back to shore and flopped onto my back. Saltwater coursed over me, splashing my face as I made angels in the sand. Bree joined me, with Sen on my other side. Vera jumped in the water wearing the bikini she had on under her clothes. Bree jumped in after Vera but not before shooting me a knowing look. She was so on to me.

Sen took my hand and stood, pulling me into the ocean with her. She pulled me deeper, so that each wave went over our heads. When I came up for air, I'm nearly positive her smile glowed in the dark.

We treaded water, looking deep into each other's eyes. Electricity rushed down to my hands and feet, and suddenly everything around us muted. All I heard was our laughter and the immediate sounds of water lapping at my

Jaz Joyner

skin. This was bliss. I waded for a moment with Sen by my side. We laughed when a huge wave enveloped me and I went under. I wasn't afraid, more like excited. The water settled a bit and my heart rate slowed again.

I pulled away from Sen and closer to shore. I had returned to reality without meaning to but bliss was still my mood. I tried to smooth my curls, with no success. Sen allowed herself to float away a few feet, and I just watched, content. Vera trudged out behind me, then Bree. Sen was the last.

I whispered, *Thank you,* to the ocean. Sen made her way over to me and her foot got stuck in sand. We all erupted with laughter. That is, until a quick-moving light illuminated our hang out. My eyes followed the light to a figure holding a flashlight.

"Hey!" I heard the figure say, and that was all it took for us to hightail out of there, stopping just long enough to grab our clothes. Two patrol officers wildly waving flashlights emerged from the road to the beach through the inky dark. We kept running towards The Hole. I could hear Bree and Vera whooping loudly as they caught up behind us. I raced as fast as I could on pure adrenaline and bare feet. I stopped, seeing lights flash behind us. We'd beaten them. I slowed down right at The Hole's entrance.

Sen leaned on the side of the building and huffed, "Good. We lost them."

Her gaze was unwavering. I usually would have retreated like a hermit, but I didn't mind it. I stared right back.

"Oh my god, I haven't run that fast in forever," Vera exhaled.

I plopped on the ground and pulled on my jeans.

"That was crazy." Bree said, and it made me laugh so hard. I, Juniper Bray, almost got in trouble for trespassing.

"We seriously almost got caught!" I cackled. I stood and pulled my shirt over my head.

Vera sniffed her dress before putting it on, "I smell like seaweed. I'm going home and taking like two showers."

She combed her fingers through her damp hair, turning to leave.

Bree stopped her and blurted, "Hey! June's birthday is comin' up soon!"

I was stunned Bree even knew my birthday. It was exactly one month away. Vera's eyebrows shot up, and she stopped short.

Sen touched my shoulder, "Really?"

"Yeah," I scratched the back of my neck and face. I had a feeling a hangout plan was coming up and I was not ready.

"Do you want to hang out then? We could have a little party." I'd never seen Vera so excited, and she was already pretty animated.

Sen leaned into me. I thought she was about to kiss me, but instead she whispered, "Vera loves birthdays."

An epic tease.

Everyone's eyes were on me, so I stammered, "Yeah. That would be really cool."

My stomach fluttered. I knew my parents liked to spend my birthday with me so I wasn't quite sure how the whole "party" idea would work out, especially since our moms weren't fans of Sen or Vera. But I didn't let myself stress on the details. I focused on the fact that I'd get to see Sen again, and soon. Sen grabbed her skateboard suddenly.

"Sounds good. See you then?"

She swung her skateboard onto her shoulder, and I clamped my mouth shut so it wouldn't gape open. Everything she did was dope.

"Yeah, for sure," I said, because that's how I assumed an equally cool person would respond.

If I were assertive enough, I would have kissed her, but I wasn't, and we didn't. She bent down and gave me a hug that ended too soon, then waved to everyone, hopped on her skateboard, and took off into the night.

"Somebody's got a crush," Vera teased.

I didn't even care that she was trying to make fun of me. I was still in a trance. I just smiled to myself.

"Okay, well, peace, girls. See you!" Vera waltzed off.

The sound of the ocean was constant. My body tingled.

"That was fun, huh?" Bree asked me.

Juniper Leaves

"It was..." I said.

Bree said, "We should go, too. It's 2 a.m."

"We should."

We headed toward the spot where we'd arrived. I focused on Bree's bedroom, and we were quickly sucked into a portal.

We arrived in the middle of the living room, so, okay, a little off, but not bad! It was dark and quiet, and a rush of relief overcame me. We tiptoed upstairs, and I wondered what Sen might be thinking about. I imagined she was thinking of me, of the night, just like I was.

I thought of my grandma always telling me she saw spunk in me. I didn't really believe her until then. Maybe it was just a moment of inflated confidence, maybe I was high off of my crush. That night I didn't care what it was, I felt good.

CHAPTER ELEVEN

"Breana, come with me," was the first thing I heard when arriving in Cantatis that morning.

A sentence I hadn't expected, simply because I thought the whole point of Bree and me being a team meant we had to stay together. I stood there, confused, as Bree followed Aggro off into the forest until I couldn't see them anymore. The time to battle was coming soon, yet I hadn't learned to fight, and I wouldn't, at least not in the way most people understand it. Bree, would become a warrior with Aggro, while I stayed with Harmonia and learned something I didn't quite comprehend yet.

Our next few times in Cantatis, we'd arrive and immediately go our separate ways: Bree off to fight training and me with Harmonia.

That particular morning was the first of this odd change in flow, and I had all the questions, "I thought we were supposed to stay together? Why aren't we both training in the same things?"

Harmonia had me sit, then, on a rock by a creek in the middle of the woods of Cantatis. She warned me that the next thing she'd say may be off-putting.

"Juniper, you won't fight with your fists, you will fight with your mind. You have a power you've not yet channeled, one Breana doesn't share. That's what you will begin to learn today."

Of course I had a million more questions:

What sort of mind fighting am I supposed to do?

Why didn't you tell me this before?

Have I always had this power?

But all that came out was, "How?"

She responded to me with another question, "How do you want to win this war?"

I was sitting in a whirlwind of confusion. I had no idea how I wanted to win the war, let alone if that was even the sort of question I should be answering. How do I even have the power to answer that?

As if reading my mind, Harmonia said, "You are worthy of this question, Juniper. You, in fact, will be the one to face the greatest threat in our final battle. The Ambassador always does. So for your training, we will challenge your mind, and your body will follow."

Harmonia instructed me to stand and then told me, "Say anything. Whatever comes to your mind."

"I miss Grandma." I said, a thought constantly at the center of my thoughts.

Harmonia said nothing for too long. Long enough for the thought to rattle inside my brain and force a tear down my face.

Then, when the noise around me grew so quiet I could only hear my own breath, she said, "Tell me a fond memory you have of your grandmother."

I wiped the lone tear from my chin. I didn't need time to think of a moment, but I sat silent anyway, reliving my favorite time with my grandmother. I was eleven, and I'd just butchered a volcano presentation for science class because I'd forgotten to bring my notes. I probably wasn't as horrible as I thought I was, but all that mattered was that I was freaking out inside. When Ms. Wright escorted me out of the classroom to "collect myself" I asked if I could call someone. She said yes, and so I called my grandma. I told Grandma how I started crying in front of my entire class and couldn't even finish my presentation, which we both knew I worked so hard on. I told her I did a horrible job, and I was so mad at myself.

I'll never forget what she said to me, "It's okay to be disappointed, Juniper. You worked hard on that project, and it is absolutely fine to be unhappy with how it turned out. But let me tell you something. You are a brilliant girl. But you know what? You don't owe no proof of that to nobody. So those kids didn't see how great you are in that presentation. Does that make you any less great? Does that make you any less marvelous? If the kids don't think you're phenomenal, does that make you less wonderful? Simply by existing, you are proving to everyone how wonderful you are, because Juniper, you really are that wonderful. Do you know that?"

She waited for me to say yes, and it took a long, long time. But when I finally did, I meant it. My grandma always had a way of uplifting like no one else could.

"After talks with her, I would feel like the strongest, most brilliant girl in the world."

I walked with Harmonia leading the way through the forest. She looked back at me and asked, "Do you feel that way now? Strong? Brilliant?"

I knew how I needed to answer, but didn't feel that way at all.

"I don't know," I said finally, scratching my chin.

I wanted the words to flow out of me like water: *Of course I'm strong and brilliant and great!*

"I see you have not yet found the confidence your grandmother saw in you. That I cannot change. However, Juniper, I challenge you to start believing. When the battle nears its end, it will not be swords, or knives, or arrows that will win. It will be your mind. The mind your grandmother always knew was destined for great things."

Many of my training days went like this. I'd arrive with Harmonia, and she would ask me difficult questions like:

"What is something you know to be true?"

Or:

"When was the last time you felt strong?"

And I would respond with what I hoped were good answers, even if I didn't fully believe them. But she never accepted my first answer. She'd ask again and again, until I'd pause and really think about what I'd say next. I'd leave feeling introspective. That confidence I'd searched for all my life wasn't only something I wanted, but something I needed now, and I wasn't quite sure where I'd find it. I wasn't quite sure how my grandma even knew it was in me somewhere to begin with.

My last day of training, we didn't meet in the forest. We didn't really meet at all, if we're being technical. I arrived on the sandy lavender beaches of Cantatis and saw Bree off, as she jogged away, practice sword in tow. She'd bragged to me about how dope she was with a sword. I remember watching her disappear into the woods and noticing how envious felt. I had been training just as long as her, but didn't really feel I had anything to show for it.

I sat in the sand and waited for Harmonia. Time came and went as I paced the beach and looked into the water, hoping she'd somehow flow out of it, but nothing. The waves grew stronger and I didn't pay them much mind at first. They grew louder and bigger until their size left me unsettled. I backed away only to run fully when I realized the waves were chasing me.

The voice of a monster yelled to me, "Run. Yes. Run! You fearful child!"

I sprinted. I glanced back, and the wave had become its own entity, separate from the ocean. A twelve-foot-tall watery, fluid creature chased me through the sand. As I neared the forest, I ran into some sort of invisible barrier. I turned around to face the creature, who was uncomfortably close to me now. It was huge, ominous even, but I realized I wasn't afraid. It hovered over me in all its monstrosity, but all I saw was water. I knew water. I could swim, I could hold my breath longer than most. Water was never a monster to me.

I closed my eyes and imagined the softness of the ocean, the parts I felt at home in, and I yelled, "Enough!"

I kept my eyes closed and yelled it again, louder this time.

"Enough!"

I heard the roar of the waves encircling me. I refused to watch this happen so I could stay focused on this strong feeling. *You are not afraid of water.*

One more time, I said, "Enough! I'm not afraid of you!"

The creature stopped its noisy circling. I couldn't hear the rush of the waves anymore. I opened my eyes to find the creature shrinking in front of me, slowly revealing what was inside: Harmonia. Harmonia, the one whom I'd just told about my love of the water just one training day ago. The one who knew the ocean was one of the few things I never feared. The one who knew that deep, deep in me, somewhere, was a sort of strength only my grandmother saw for so many years.

"Good."

She fluttered towards me, as the rest of the ocean made its way back home. She didn't need to say anything else. I knew what I'd been training for now. My power was of the mind. I can stare a monster right in its face and make it stop; I can dominate it, make it submit to me, but only if I believed I could. And believing would be the hardest part for me.

CHAPTER TWELVE

I first heard about Sweet Sixteens when I was five. Rich friends of Dad's turned their basement into a laser tag arena for their teenage son. They invited the entire school, including the kids my age. There was a bounce house for people my age, a bar for the adults, and lifeguards at the pool in the backyard.

"Now this is a party," Dad joked while eyeing the stack of presents in the Mom's arms that reached up to her ears.

It wasn't until I got older that I learned most kids aspired to have parties like this on their sixteenth birthday. I mean, Sweet Sixteen was a whole show on MTV for a while. And not that I care about the capitalist parts of birthdays. I don't really care about presents or big parties or anything that involves social interaction with more than three people at a time. For me, it's the meaning behind the birthday that really gets me. The fact that it's a "coming-of-age" day. It's supposed to be that special day, that "not a girl, not yet a woman" time, like in that Britney Spears song. But for me, I knew, just like every other birthday, I'd feel the same. At least, I thought I would. Every year, I'd wake up that sunny birthday morning and look and feel exactly how I did the day before. Birthdays for me were reminders of how quiet my life was. Reminders that I wasn't too keen on adventure and my birthday itself would probably be the most excitement I'd experience all that year.

But this year was different. I'd already experienced more excitement than I had in my entire life in less than three months. Plus, sixteen was not just an age for me: it would be the day of the most difficult battle of my life. I'd have until sunset to arrive in Cantatis and even though the rest of my day would be free, I knew it would be all I could think about. I was scared and hesitant, but no level of worrying would stop the day from coming. My fear was contrasted by my parents' oblivious excitement.

"We're going to go above and beyond for June's birthday this year. One of the benefits of being the only kid in the house, huh, Junebug?"

He was right. Birthdays up until then were a whole production for us. My mom wrapped her arm around me.

"We came up with the best plan," she said, stroking my hair.

"We're throwin' you a combination party," my dad chimed in.

"It'll be a sort of going-away, coming-of-age situation," Uncle Robbie added.

"Your favorite holiday, right, June?" Dad said.

His eager face was difficult to match, though I tried. Birthdays really were my favorite holiday. They were the only days in my year that I knew for a fact there'd be something thrilling in store. The year before, my parents took me on a surprise day trip to the American Museum of Natural History in New York after I'd mentioned in passing to them how much I'd always wanted to go. They had no idea I'd written about AMNH's new Mummy Exhibit in my journal months before. The joy from last year simply wouldn't come to me though. Each time I'd think about Sweet Sixteen I'd be clouded by the nerve-racking reality of my upcoming battle. So I put on my tepid grin and said, "Yeah, it's gonna be great."

"You're so spoiled," Bree grumbled.

I glared at her, even though I knew she was probably right. One of my very first memories was of my sixth birthday, when they took me to a petting zoo, along with a bunch of kids I used to play with from our local playground. On my eighth birthday, my dad took me fossil digging where we found the rare fern fossil I never travel without, and even brought with me to Evershire. Another year, my parents planned a whole family vacation to the Smithsonian Museums in D.C., where we spent the day visiting every exhibit we had time for. Every year was like this.

I wondered if I would grow out of my parents doing this for me. Maybe this year would be the last time. Maybe next year I would grow out of this. My birthday was nearly here and each day prior I'd marked an X on my calendar filled with apprehension.

"Let's go out tonight," Bree suggested, as I sipped water from a mason jar at the kitchen table.

To call my expression a "deer in headlights" was probably an understatement.

"Tonight?" I repeated.

She washed her bowl in the sink, looked back at me, and said, "You know we're gonna go into battle tomorrow, right? And we were gonna meet up with Sen and Vera anyway remember?"

"Yeah, but I was thinking that would be in broad day like, like *after* we're done fighting for our lives." I put the mason jar down, suddenly feeling tense.

Of course I wanted to see Sen and hang out one last time before leaving Evershire, but it felt sacrilege to go out before our battle in Cantatis. It was like celebrating before winning the big game. Bree shrugged and turned off the faucet, then muttered what I'd hoped neither of us would say out loud, "I dunno about you, but I don't want to die without getting lit just one more time."

I felt a particularly superstitious need to counteract what she'd just said.

"We're not going to die!" I whispered too loudly.

I repeated it again softer now, even though I was still shouting inside. Doubt had a firm grip on me. I knew we'd be in danger in Cantatis. Of course. I knew we could die, too, but it's not something I allowed myself to think about for more than a millisecond at a time. I knew that Grandma had done just what I was doing and she made it through her teens, but I was no Alice Jackson. Before Evershire, I was basically on autopilot and all of a sudden the weight of the world was on my shoulders. Bree was right, but I wasn't ready to admit it.

"I don't know," is all I said.

I was feeling every bit of fear and thinking about the many ways the Mutabo could off me, but still all I said was "I don't know," because if I'd said anymore she would have seen right through me. Maybe she already did.

She hushed to almost a whisper and leaned in close to me. He eyes were sincere, "We can win this, June. We can. But wouldn't it be great to celebrate living just one more time before this all goes down? Think about it."

And then she left me there with my thoughts. I remembered Sen calling me out on my "safe" life, and even though it was a joke, I hadn't let it go. Everything about me outside of Cantatis was as "safe" as it ever was.

My grandmother used to tell me, "You've got a spark in you, just waiting to get out!"

I always cringed when she said that, because I couldn't find that spark she was talking about. I saw it for just a moment in the ocean, though, and that's why I decided I had to go with Bree that night. I had to feel it at least one more time before I battled for the world.

I set my mason jar in the sink marched upstairs.

I swung Bree's door open and I demanded, "Let's do it."

"Yes!?" Bree beamed at the edge of her bed. She continued,

"How you wanna do this, Juniper Bray?"

I fumbled for what to say next, since I, for whatever reason, thought things would just be decided after I said my thing.

"Let's like, go to a club or something."

She giggled. My face went hot with embarrassment. I realized I didn't really know what "going out" looked like for people that weren't me and Grandma.

"You really wanna do this? I'm so excited. If you're serious, I'll text Sen and Vera. They go to 'the club' all the time."

She giggled again and I couldn't help but laugh at myself. I knew nothing about being a chill teen. I took a deep breath and steadied myself for seeing Sen again. The thought of being face-to-face with her again gave me all sorts of butterflies.

That afternoon, Bree and I met with Aggro once more at the silver beach. We were supposed to learn about one more elusive non-fighting, fighting technique they'd told us about.

"Please sit. I have news," they told us as soon as we got there.

Something in their voice made my neck tense up.

"We've found the Mutabo's motivation in interfering with your family. I fear it's an unsettling discovery. Your parents' alterations of the Valeferus hold a special power for the Mutabo. You see, currently only leaders of the Mutabo can take over human bodies, and only for a few hours at a time. With the Valeferus plant, along with their own dark magic, not only can the whole Mutabo race take over human bodies, they can do so indefinitely. The Mutabo cannot survive on Earth on their own. Your father's discovery is their only hope."

I tightened my hands into fists. I was shaking too much to focus. Fragmented questions swirled in my head. I thought of my dad and Auntie Elaine, of my mom and the McKinneys, and every human who had no idea the danger they were in.

"There is good news, though. The Mutabo planet is dying fast. Instead of possessing your mother's actual body, now they've simply copied her outer shell with weak magic. We have learned where they keep her during the moments they are on Earth."

"So my mom isn't even on Earth right now?"

I heard the fear in her voice.

"Well, we imagine she is on Earth now, but she will be taken soon for at least hours at a time. There are Mutabo protecting the lair where your mother stayed at all times. We will have to wait. Do not stray far from each other tomorrow. Juniper, on the day of your birth, you must find this serum your parents have created and return it to Cantatis when you arrive for battle. You will be most powerful then and must arrive at exactly sundown if we expect any chance of beating these monsters. We will contain the serum here and return it to your parents when the battle is over. You cannot allow the Mutabo to get it. In the meantime, we will be preparing here at Cantatis, and I suggest you prepare as well. This battle will not be easy, but we can win if we are truly ready."

Before I could stop myself, I asked, "Do you think we're ready?"

Without hesitation, Aggro walked close to me and asked, "The question is: Do you?"

Aggro and Bree looked at me with ardent expressions. I didn't know what to say. Was I ready? Were we ready? I wasn't convinced. Though I'd been training so often, I still felt there was more I should know, and maybe I'd always feel that way. We were sent back to North Carolina, USA, Earth—a place that, if we weren't prepared, humankind would soon not be a part of. We were told to return to Cantatis at sundown the next day, my birthday. Which would be around the same time everyone would gather around a fire pit to start my party. I couldn't even think about how we'd manage that.

"Continue to ask yourself that question. Remember, the answer lies within."

With that, Aggro nodded, and we vanished in the wind, back to Bree's bedroom.

In the farthest corners of my mind, the thought of battle hung around like an unwelcomed guest. At the forefront was my night with Sen, Vera and Bree. We planned to teleport into town after midnight so we'd avoid the risk of waking up our parents. The more I thought about our night, the more resolved I became. I wanted to feel free. I wanted to feel as alive as I did at the ocean.

That morning as I fed the pigs, Wilbur told me, "Don't be afraid. If you believe you can defeat them, you shall."

Wilbur hadn't said much in so long that his words felt more like an omen then a simple pep talk. I wanted to believe things were fine, that we would win. But then again, I never really understood people who were one hundred percent confident about anything. My grandmother would have told me I was getting in my own way.

"How can I do that?" I asked him, as if I really thought he'd have the answer. Or if he did have the answers, like he'd even tell me, or I'd understand.

"Believe in yourself," he repeated.

If they were supposed to be motivating, his words had the opposite effect on me. Being told to believe made me believe less; being instructed to look within made me rely on external evidence. I started to walk away more unsure.

"Juniper!" He shouted after at me.

I didn't look back.

The rest of the day was a blur. I remember eating dinner, having a forgettable conversation with Uncle Robbie about his time in L.A.. I checked my watch and it read 11:30 p.m., and I wondered where the rest of the day had gone. The house was dark and quiet, and the fact that I'd be sixteen in just minutes sunk in like a heavy weight on my chest.

"Let me give you a makeover!" Bree shrieked, as she closed the bedroom door.

She sounded more like a bubble-gum teen than I'd ever heard her sound before.

"I don't know, I don't really wear a lot of makeup well."

When I was twelve, I could pass for eight, and at nearly sixteen, I didn't look a day over twelve and a half. I didn't want to embarrass myself.

Bree looked like she was about to burst, "Pleeeeeeeease!"

"Okay," I shrugged, like it was no big deal but inside I grew nervous unsure how I'd rock a full face of makeup. I really wanted to wear it, but didn't want to be noticed for wearing it even more. I know that's silly but I didn't want to stand out or look like I was trying too hard. Bree, on the other hand, wore dark eyeliner and unnatural-colored lipsticks, like blue and black, like a uniform, and it looked so effortless on her.

I sat in front of the bathroom mirror as Bree transformed me into a smoky eyed young adult.

"Whoa…"

I definitely didn't look like I was trying too hard. I felt like I was about to walk the red carpet.

"Where you goin'?"

I swiveled around to find Robbie Jr. leaning on the bathroom door with his arms folded, looking nosy per usual. Bree hissed at him to get out, but he just smiled and settled into the door frame.

"Not till you tell me what you're doing."

I sucked my teeth at his smugness.

"None of your business, that's what," Bree said.

"Well, if you don't tell me, I'm telling Ma y'all are trying to sneak out of the house."

I wracked my brain for a casual explanation, something believable enough, but I came up with nothing. I looked up at Bree for inspiration, but her face was as blank as mine. I stood out of my chair and looked him in the eye.

"I have twenty dollars left." I assured him.

He scrunched up his face, "Twenty? I don't need your money. I'm telling, this bout to be too funny."

It was the only money I had from an allowance I'd gotten weeks ago, before even getting to North Carolina. He waved his hands dismissively.

He laughed, "Ma's gonna be so mad at y'all," and started to walk away.

Ugh.

"Wait!" Bree shouted back at him.

I scratched my arm. I felt my full face of makeup start to sweat.

"I'll do the chores on the barn for a month. Pinky swear." Bree promised.
Robbie Jr. stopped midway on the stairs and started coming back up, slowly.

"That's stupid. But I mean, if you really want to." He said.

Robbie let out his pinky and then pulled it away. With his pinky in the air he looked directly at me. I was confused at first, and then saw in his expression, he wanted more. My eyes tried to bargain with him but he wouldn't back down.

"Fine." I said. I thought quick on my feet.

I hurried to my nightstand, grabbed the fossil my dad gave me, and handed it to Robbie, "Here."

"June, come on—"

Bree tried to interject, but I gave it anyway.

Robbie lit up, "What is it?"

"It's a really rare plant fossil. It's hundreds of thousands of years old. I found it with my dad and he says it'll probably be worth a lot one day."

I knew I was doing what I had to do. I couldn't take any chances. We couldn't get caught. That's all I could think about. I wouldn't let myself think about how much I already regretted it.

He studied it for what felt like eons, "Really rare?"

I nodded.

Finally, he said, "Cool," and walked away.

I felt devastated but relieved.

I sighed deeply, "Your brother is the worst..."

"Yeah, I know..." Bree agreed.

I turned away. Strong emotions fought each other on my face. I felt guilty for giving up my fossil but there was more at stake than the loss of a precious gift. I didn't want anyone to see how sad I was about the fossil. It was the sort of gift I thought I'd cherish forever, and I'd lost it in seconds. I felt guilty for giving it up so quickly. I tried reminding myself how important that night was.

I had to do it, I told myself. *I had to.*

Bree let me borrow the only "club-worthy" clothing item she owned that fit me: a black tube dress. Not something I'd ever wear on my own, and the tightness of it was a feeling I'd never experienced. Still, I was excited. I felt cute and mature. Bree stretched my hair into a big fro and instructed me to wear my black Doc Marten boots. They were the nicest shoes I'd brought with me. Most days, I would have been a fish out of water in that outfit, but that night, I was perfect.

Bree smoothed her green hair — which had grown a little to reveal her dark roots — down with hair whip and a wave brush. She put on black platform heels that made her look like a giant next to me, and wore tight jeans and a t-shirt with *STFU* emblazoned across the front.

"I told my parents I got rid of this a long time ago," she said and laughed, "But I kept it for nights like this."

With her black lipstick and nails, she didn't look much different than any other day, but her vibe was different. I always knew Bree was the in-your-face, take-it-or-leave it type but that night she wasn't standing out to stand out, she was just shining in a way that made it impossible for her not to. I returned to the mirror once more, worried the whole Robbie fiasco may have smudged my makeup. It hadn't one bit, I still looked fresh and clean and glamorous. I fluffed my hair and stared at the smoky eyed girl staring back at me. I looked beautiful if I do say so myself. I felt my age, for the first time ever. I was an adventurous 16-year-old ready for a night on the town. That's what I told myself in the mirror, and what I whole-heartedly believed as I exited the bathroom with a smile on my face.

"Okay, one more thing," Bree dug inside her dresser drawer and pulled out a clear plastic bag.
She dipped her hand in and pulled out three IDs, "Happy birthday."

The IDs had pictures of three different black women, none of whom looked like me. Bree took the middle one, which belonged to an older woman, at least in her thirties, wearing a pink-collared shirt. I settled on one where the woman had a vaguely similar afro to mine.

"Is this even gonna work?"

Bree shrugged, "It does for me."

We crept down the stairs at a snail's pace. My heart stopped twice each time Bree's heavy heels clunked on stairs on the way down. Somehow we made it through the front door without getting caught. I wasn't the same that night. Something was very different; I felt in control. I kept smiling to myself. The portal felt different, too. I was stronger in its presence, as it effortlessly opened when Bree and I linked hands. I closed my eyes as we stepped through, imagining the picture of the bar Bree had shown me on her phone.

We came out the other side into an obscure alleyway. If it weren't for the loud music playing not too far from us, I'd have thought we were off track. We followed the frenzy of voices, and the electronic beat pulsed through my skin, down to my bones. Strobe lights surged through the doorway the closer we got. There was no line, and a bouncer barely glanced at our identification before letting us stroll right in. The physical space between one person to the next was laughable.

"Bree!" Sen shouted in a fleeting moment of quiet between songs.

Bree and I squeezed past the scent of cologne and sweat to get to Sen and Vera sitting several feet from us in a lounge area.

"Did ya'll take a cab?" Sen shouted over the music.

I fished around for a believable response before Bree saved me.

"What're you drinking?" She pointed to the can in Sen's hand.

"A Modelo!" Sen raised the can and took a swig.

I shouted, "How'd you get those?"

"These!" Vera flashed a driver's license of a strawberry-blond woman three times her age, wearing a turtleneck and a staid expression.

"Now let's get us some shots!"

Vera linked her arm in mine and led all of us through the crowd, up to the bar. She asked for four lemon drops. I didn't know much about alcohol. I pushed my nerves down and put on a brave face. *Tonight is my night.*

"On the house, sweetie." The bartender said with a sleazy grin.

After putting the necessary ingredients together, he slid us four sugar-rimmed, yellow shots with an unsolicited wink. I shuddered. Vera batted her eyes at the bartender like it was nothing and thanked him.

She shrugged and whispered to me, "At least they're free!"

"To June," Bree said, as we all raised our shots in the air.

Sen and everyone said happy birthday to me. My face got hot and I grinned in spite of myself.

Vera turned toward the bar.

"Can we get another round?" She sweetly asked the creepy bartender.

He nodded and in under a minute slid us four more. They were sweet and bitter and delicious but the alcohol was absolutely apparent.

I asked Bree, "Are shots always this strong?"

She put her hand on my shoulder and smirked, "Not when you get drunk."

We had two more rounds courtesy of Vera and headed to the dance floor. I grew more loose with each shot, and by the third, I was as wavy as an air dancer. I got in sync with the deep bass filling the room. My eyelids drooped, and I swayed freely in time with the music, as euphoric dancing strangers moved in unison around me. A warm, sticky arm wrapped around my waist, and I turned to find Sen gazing down at me again with those hypnotic eyes.

She shouted something.

"What?" I shouted back

"Are you having a good time?"

I planned to say *You have no idea*, but what came out was, "Dance with me."

I felt confident and self-assured. She did as I said. I relished the warmth of Sen's breath on my shoulder, as we swayed close to each other. It only lasted for a moment, though, because on came Vera, the ruiner of moments.

"Let's go outside!" she shouted, right in my ear.

Sen let go of me, and I wobbled a bit not realizing I was leaning on her so much.

"Right now?" Sen asked.

She seemed disappointed.

"Yeah, my cousin's out there waitin' for us."

I didn't know what this meant. As if Vera's cousin was someone special we were all supposed to know. But still, we filed out of the club to the back alley to meet him. Bree danced a couple bodies away by herself. When we caught her eye, she cheered drunkenly over the music. Vera waved her over.

Sen held the door for me as I stumbled outside. I felt loose still, but instead of floating now, I just wobbled like a weeble toy. Vera raised her eyebrows while pantomiming smoking, glancing from face to face to gauge interest. As drunk as I was, I wondered if this was a good idea, considering my first encounter with weed.

"You wanna smoke?" Sen asked me.

I wanna go back inside and dance. I'm having fun with you, I thought.

"Yeah!" I yelled instead.

I vowed to tell her how I felt soon, very soon.

A lanky teen boy, who was smoking while wearing a bucket hat, waved at the four of us, "Hi, ya'll. I'm Ruben. I'm sure you've heard everything about me!"

His thick, black eyebrows rippled as he excitedly introduced himself. He and Vera had the same nose, despite strikingly different features elsewhere. Pimples cluttered his cheeks, and his goofy stance made him seem younger than us. The lemon shots were still going strong in my bloodstream, and I didn't mind one bit. But then everything began to spin. I tried to focus my eyes as my vision blurred.

I leaned into Sen and let my head rest on her shoulder. Without hesitation, she put her arm around mine. I snuggled in. I thought I might fall asleep.

Ruben took a joint from behind his ear and passed it to Vera, who lit it and puffed. She passed it to Bree, who shook her head.

Vera nodded to her, "Go'on then! That's good stuff."

Bree held it loosely in her fingers and firmly said, "Nah, I get weird when I drink and smoke at the same time."

She went over to sit cross-legged on the pavement. Vera rolled her eyes and passed the joint to me.

Brazen and getting drunker by the minute, I eagerly toked on the joint, mimicking how Vera did it to look as authentic as possible. Immediately, I started coughing again, only this time huge grey-blue clouds of smoke billowed out of my lungs. My eyes watered, mascara tracks forming on my face.

"You alright?" Sen asked, patting me on the back.

I said, "Yeah, of course," between chokes.

I wiped my eyes and nodded as the coughing eased up.

When the joint came around again, Bree said, "Maybe that's enough?"

I laughed and shouted, "Live a little! Isn't that what you always say?"

Everyone laughed, except Bree. I was on a roll.

Sen raised the joint in the air, "To living," and took the deepest drag I had ever seen.

Vera and Ruben did the same. When it was my turn again, I passed. I was ready to dance. I was uninhibited, and the words flew out of me,

"Do you want to dance with me instead? I need to get in there and shake this alcohol out of my body. It's my birthday, I wanna have fun!" I slurred.

I didn't know I slurred then, but I definitely slurred. I grabbed Sen's hand and led us inside, like a femme fatale. I felt powerful.

We parked at a tiny opening among the crowd and danced wildly to the music. I put my arms around her waist. I swished my hips and smiled up at her, and our eyes met.

I yelled, "I really like you!"

"What?" She shouted back.

And I said it again, because I had no inhibitions: "I really like you!"

I tightened my arms around her. She leaned in, and time stood still.

"I like you, too," she said in my ear.

I'll never forget how good those words felt floating through my mind. Her lips got closer and closer to mine and grazed me just a little. I was more wobbly than before and I didn't care. I squeezed Sen tighter to keep myself balanced. I was tingly all over though I wasn't sure if that was my drunkenness or infatuation with Sen. I felt dizzy even though I was barely moving. Bile rose in my throat. I cleared my throat, fighting an unbeatable fight.

"I think I'm gonna be sick," I said and scrambled off the dance floor.

The taste of lemons and sugar filled my mouth.

Sen rushed to my side and asked, "What did you say? I couldn't hear—"

She was too close. There was no time. I couldn't hold it anymore and threw up all over her. I stepped back as fast as I could but I was in a daze, as if moving quickly would change what had just happened.

"I'm so sorry!" I squealed, words smearing together.

I stumbled to the bar and grabbed wads of napkins. I staggered back to Sen and tried to wipe her off. She backed away from me like I was carrying a disease.

I apologized again and again, more times that I can count, "Sen, I'm sor—"

I teetered as I stood up, still holding the soiled wads of napkins. I'm sure I looked gross. I felt gross.

"It's fine." Her expression said otherwise. She straightened her shirt and pressed past me without looking at me, "I'm gonna go to the bathroom."

It was torture watching her leave. Bree, Vera, and Ruben made their way to me as Sen closed the bathroom door.

"Oh shit!" Vera exclaimed.

Having them discover what just happened was like I had to relive it. Vera and Ruben couldn't stop giggling. Bree looked at me with all sorts of pity, and I couldn't tell which was worse. Their giggles built until they were rolling in laughter, too high to be concerned with my mess. My ears were ringing. My legs were giving out. Bree caught me before I collapsed on the floor.

"We're leaving now," said Bree over the buzzing noise in my head.

I didn't want to leave on such a sour note without redeeming myself.

I teetered towards the bathroom, "I have to apologize to Sen."

"No, you're a hot ass mess, like for real. We're leaving," Bree caught me again, because I must have been falling.

"I've gotta find Sen. I've got to."

I was losing my mind. I kept rambling about Sen, while Bree pushed me closer to the exit. Sen must have been disgusted by me. In my drunken state, I was convinced if I could find her one more time, I could prove I wasn't a total loser.

"Come on. You look like shit right now."

"You look like shit!" I blurted out.

Vera and her cousin kept laughing behind us somewhere, or that's the way my brain replays this memory.

"Sen! Sen!" I shouted, as Bree scanned the street outside the club.

Bree gritted her teeth, "Stop! We have to find the nearest portal!"

"Why would I know where that is? I dunno," I slurred.

Bree later told me I started mumbling nonsense at this point. So the next thing she said was, "Fuck. We'll have to take a cab."

Understandably so. She nearly carried me up the street, where a taxi sat on the side of the road, my arm around her shoulder, and my head swinging back and forth like a rag doll. She shoved me in the cab and got in behind me.

We pulled away from the curb, swerving harshly around the corner, or at least that's what it felt like in my drunken mind.

The journey home was like my first ride in a spaceship. Many millennia later, the driver pulled into the farm and jerked to a stop.

"We don't have any money!" I mumbled too loudly.

"What are you talking about! Yes we do!" Bree looked frustrated. She rummaged around in her pocket looking for change we both knew wasn't there.

The cab driver tapped his long nails on the steering wheel. I feel nauseous again. *Oh no.* I opened the cab door just in time to barf on my leg and boot.

"Sir, I need to get my friend inside, I swear I'll come back out with your money. Is that okay? " Bree sounded so adult. I laughed to myself, not realizing how much shit we'd just gotten ourselves into.

"Fine. Hurry up." The cab driver said, reluctantly. Bree got out and came over to my side of the cab. She made me put my arm around her and helped me inside. I felt like I weighed a ton and I smelled disgusting. I stumbled into the house and sat on the first step because I didn't feel like moving anymore.

"June, where's that 20 dollars you have?" She asked me.

I heard her but I couldn't think clearly. I must have murmured something because she said,

"What are you talking about?"

I shrugged. She ran upstairs for a moment and came down with money in her hand. Even with my twenty dollars it wouldn't be enough for a 40-minute cab ride but I wished for the best. She went back outside and I stayed where I was, wavy, on the brink of my third upchuck. She came back in looking distraught. She quietly closed the door behind her and I noticed she still had the money in her hand.

"Do you have any other money with you?" Bree paced back and forth.

Suddenly the light from the cab lights went out. I tried standing up to see what was going on. I sat right back down. Bree backed away from the door and stood at the bottom of the stairs, frozen, as if that would make her invisible. I was nearly drunk enough to believe it would. I was also drunk enough to stand again just to see for myself. The man with his black, collared shirt and khakis pounded on the front door, and I wished for a simpler time when I had no friends.

I felt faint again. Bree paced back and forth again. And then we weren't alone anymore. Uncle Robbie stepped out of his bedroom in pajamas and slippers and a tired frown.

"What is all this noise about?" he demanded.

Auntie was right behind him, followed by Mom and Dad. This really was the end for us. I didn't need to be sober to understand that.

CHAPTER THIRTEEN

Bree and I waited as Mom paid the cab fare, and then she told us to sit down. She sat at the chair opposite me in the kitchen, like a detective. My dad wouldn't even look at me, and he was right next to her.

The bags under my mom's eyes were like pillows. I was too drunk to think to apologize for waking her up.

"I'm very dizzy," I said out loud, meaning for it just to be a thought.

Bree nudged me, so I dramatically tried to straighten myself up without success.

"Have you been drinking?" My mom asked me.

I hesitated, "Um..."

My eyes were unable to focus. Bree put her face in her palms.

My dad checked his watch, "It is three in the morning."

He leaned back in his chair.

"Damn near the sun's almost come up," Uncle Robbie rubbed his temples.

"I know," was all Bree could say.

Was all I think I would have said, if I could even think straight. My fossil was sitting in the middle of the table, and it already had a noticeable nick in it. *Dammit, Junior.* I grabbed it, but not before Dad noticed it sitting there. I heard footsteps on the stairs, and Junior stumbled in, rubbing his eyes.

"What's going on?" he asked.

He looked so innocent there. I was furious.

"Go to sleep," Bree and Auntie ordered at the same time.

Junior must have brought the fossil down and forgot because he stared right at me and said, "Where is it?"

My father's stare burned a hole in me when I handed it to Robbie.

"Ok, now go back to your room then, Rob," Auntie ordered.

He turned and scuttled back upstairs to his room.

"So, you gave away your fossil, too," Dad said, but I knew he didn't need me to respond. The disappointment was thick in his voice, like an inflection.

I couldn't bring myself to look at him, but I could feel him. I could feel everyone. My face was hot, and I couldn't tell if it was because I was drunk or embarrassed or both. I was so ashamed. That night was supposed to be a bold one, a fantastic one.

"June, I don't know what's gotten into you," Mom's arms were folded in front of me.

I imagined I could see myself like a fly on the wall. It didn't feel like I was actually there. I loathed feeling drunk when I needed to be sober.

"June, you better speak up," Mom must have been talking to me for a while.

"What did you say?" I asked, making things worse.

"We just hung out with some of my friends," Bree pitched in. She was somehow way more sober than I was.

Uncle Robbie asked the key question, "Which of Bree's friends did you hang with?"

Bree was quick to interject, claiming it was "nobody," which of course means somebody important. I'm very aware we were doing a horrible job.

Mom looked square at me and asked, "June, did you know these children? Bree's friends?"

"Children? I mean, they weren't really children."

I don't know why I thought it was necessary to make this distinction. Sober me wouldn't have made such a distinction.

Still, Mom ignored me and kept talking, "You're both underage. I don't know how it works in North Carolina, but as far as I'm concerned, you're a child."

"June, this just isn't like you. You know this isn't like you," Dad sounded distraught.

Instead of explaining what actually happened, I sidestepped. I got self-righteous.

"You really need to let go of this kid you think I am." My words were slurring and I didn't know it, and I sounded a lot more confident than I should have.

A vein in my mom's forehead bulged, "You've never snuck out before. You've never gotten drunk before. You've never talked back to me like this before. I mean, I don't know what you learned around here, but you are just not like that. *What* is going on?"

Auntie Elaine folded her arms, defensive, "Around here? What does that mean, around here?"

My mom's voice softened and she said,

"Nothing personal, Elaine, I just know you give Bree a lot more leeway here, but Juniper just doesn't—"

"Vivian, I'm just as shocked as you are."

"Right." Mom wouldn't even look at her.

Uh oh. The room grew tense. Even with my eyes involuntarily closing from my dizziness, I felt it. My dad walked over and put his arm around my mom.

"Vi," he said softly.

With the McKinneys sitting across from them, it visibly looked like Us vs. Them.

"I saw Bree smoking that first day, Elaine. I've heard the stories. You can't say there's no correlation here. Look at June then compared to now."

"You're unbelievable," Aunt Elaine scoffed.

A very petty part of me felt good about finally being compared to Bree as equally wild. I knew I wasn't, nor probably would I ever be, but there in my drunken state, I took pride in it. Meanwhile, Bree sat quietly beside me, like a bystander watching a train wreck. I was like the emotional equivalent of a dormant volcano about to erupt. The alcohol, the residual embarrassment from the night, I knew I was about to burst. But no one else did.

Dad spoke again, "You both could have been hurt, or worse."

His voice was soft, and his disappointment hurt me more than the anger underneath his words. And then I felt it, I was exploding. I was—

"You don't get it. I have to be fearless now. I went out to live, because I never live: I just do what everyone wants me to do. I'm tired of it. You know why I have to be fearless? Do you? My life depends on it. Your life depends on it . . . You don't get it. You think you know what I'm going through, but you don't. You have no idea!"

"June." Bree warned. The room went silent. Mom and Dad gawked at me, confusion written all over their faces. I'd never gone off like that, and sober me never would. I probably looked out of my mind.

"Juniper Alice Bray. I don't know what you're talking about, but I do know one thing. That party of yours? History—"

"Honey..." I could see my dad's heart drop. He looked more disappointed than me.

"Vivian, we've already sent out invitations—" Auntie Elaine objected.

My mom ignored her and kept talking, "And I think it would be best if we . . . Maybe stay in the city for the remainder of this trip."

Auntie stood up, "Vivian, that's highly unnecessary—"

My mom cut Auntie off again and told me to pack my things. I was dizzy as stood.

"Ma, that's too much!"

I tried to backtrack, but knew my talking back to her would lead to consequences. I knew nothing I could say would change her mind. I could never explain Cantatis to them, a paramount part of myself, a part that I thought would make me more mature. But all they saw was this child trying to be grown. And maybe they were right, maybe that's all I had been, and I just didn't realize it all this time.

I knew I was doing all of this wrong. The Juniper I wanted to be was bold and strong in a totally different way. I wish I'd known before, but it was all too late. I'd already messed so much up beyond repair.

CHAPTER FOURTEEN

I woke that morning a bloated mess, my eyes heavy with makeup and fatigue. I laid in bed like it was my coffin. I blinked several times to get my eyes adjusted, the blinding, bright yellow lights above me — nothing like the lights in Bree's bedroom. I tried to sit up and was hit with a pain in my side where I must have ran into something last night. I wiped my face only to find makeup on my hands and surveyed the foreign space. I was in a small cot on the side of a large room with a larger bed in it. The door was closed, so I walked through to find my parents in a bright and airy living room nothing like the McKinneys'. Mom made coffee in a yellow painted kitchenette, while Dad wrote something in a notebook at a glass table facing a balcony that showed the view of a beach outside.

Dad looked up at me, and his face was softer and kinder than I'd expected it to be, "Happy birthday."

Happy birthday. It was my birthday but there was nothing "happy" about it.

Mom poured herself some coffee and went to sit with my dad, and then they both studied me like a test.

"How do you feel?" My mom asked.

"Okay," I said, because I didn't want her to know I actually felt horrible in every way.

My parents wore identical expressions of weariness.

I asked, "So how long are we supposed to be here, then?"

Dad said, "Two days."

"But Dad, it's my birthday. We only have a week left."

My dad looked at me and then kept writing in his notebook.

"Dad," I pleaded. But nothing.

Finally, he said, "Juniper, you came home yesterday, but did you ever think about what could have happened? I understand it's your birthday, but you need to take a hard look at the choices that led you here right now."

I sat on an uncomfortable padded bench in pajamas that I didn't remember putting on in a hotel I didn't remember arriving at. I sat staring at my parents go about their day on what felt like a very normal Sunday, but it wasn't just any normal Sunday, it was my birthday. This was the supposed to be my "sweet" sixteen.

A dolphin clock on the wall read 3:30 p.m., which meant I had a comfortable few hours to get to Bree's, take hold of Dad's serum and head into Cantatis together by sundown. I had some brainstorming to do.

Chapter Fifteen

At least an hour later, I was still sitting on the same uncomfortable taupe bench with no plan and all the hopelessness.

Suddenly, my dad shot up like a newly energized man and said, "I'm gonna have to step out in a bit."

I perked up. I had a plan. I knew I needed to leave with him, somehow. I wasn't sure how yet, but I knew that was my best bet to stepping out of that hotel room.

Mom didn't seem happy about him taking off.

Mom asked, "Didn't you bring everything?"

"There's some extra data logs back at the farm. I thought I had them on the way here, but I must have overlooked some things."

He started packing his notebook and papers in his bag, "Maybe we could all head back a little early."

He said it passively, as if attempting to sound nonchalant made those words any less noticeable. Of course, his statement was just as loud to my mom as it would have been if he shouted it.

"No. We don't need to do that." She said quietly but assertively.

Dad leaned in to her and said, "Can we talk about this outside?"

They went out to the balcony for discretion but I still heard them.

"Vivian, I'm starting to think you're here more than just because of June."

He said my name lower than anything else. I listened closer.

"I don't see why you'd say that."

"Vi." He persisted, this time louder.

"What, are you trying to say Juniper made a good life choice yesterday? That her nearly fainting was just a little bump in the road? Being drunk at 15 is no small thing." Her voice rose with every word.

Dad glanced at me and rubbed the back of his head. I immediately played with my fingers like I wasn't listening, then had the foresight to pretend I needed water in the tiny kitchen space. The tension was unmistakable, even from there.

Mom's voice grew stronger, "I'm not the one that's been spending this whole 'vacation' hiding from my wife."

I hated hearing that when I wasn't supposed to. I knew I shouldn't eavesdrop, but at this point, it was like a train wreck. I had to. Dad raised his voice to match hers, saying she and everyone knew this was a "work trip". That working was his highest priority. I don't think he meant to sound as aloof as he did. My mom sat on a balcony chair, conveniently positioned so I could see the side of her face.

She paused for a moment, as if second-guessing herself, then said, "I needed you these past few months more than ever."

Her eyes welled up. Dad took my mom's hand. He squatted down and kissed Mom on the cheek. My dad said something to her I couldn't make out. She shook her head, wiping tears.

I looked away. I went to my room. I hated seeing them like that. I jumped when the balcony door slid open. Dad's footsteps drew closer, and I peeked out as he grabbed his bag.

I spoke timidly, "Are you leaving now?"

"I'll be back soon." He promised.

Mom repositioned the balcony chair so that she was facing the beach. I knew she was still crying. I'm sure she knew I knew. I let my dad walk out and waited for a full two minutes before following behind him, making sure to keep an eye on my mom too, in case she decided to turn around.

I slipped past the hotel's front desk into the parking lot, where three cabs sat on the curb. I wandered into the shrubbery lining the hotel, where I found a flower bed brimming with fragrant lavender. Behind them was a narrow dirt patch, just big enough for me to step into. I breathed deeply, closed my eyes, and imagined standing in the McKinney yard.

"Excuse me," I heard a voice say behind me, "What do you think you're doing here?"

I almost fell into the blooms.

"Uh, nothing!" I stammered at the gardener, trying to turn around quicker than I was able.

I hobbled out of the dirt onto the pavement.

"We don't allow anyone in the garden." He stared hard, waiting for me to respond.

"Yeah, okay. Sorry," I exhaled.

I walked around to the back of the building, then dashed across the lot in search of a private spot. I walked several blocks, but the beach town was far more crowded than any other part of quaint litter Evershire. Finally, I came across a quiet park in between two shops that was empty, except for an elderly woman who sat knitting on a bench.

I strolled as casually as I could to the back of the park, trying not to catch the woman's eye. She wasn't even paying attention. In the farthest corner, I spotted a cluster of shrubbery bordering the building that jutted up to the back of the park. I took a calming breath and looked around me one good time before I channeled the farm. I closed my eyes. I waited. And waited, until I felt the familiar gust push me into the vortex. *Yes.*

When I opened my eyes, I was in the middle of the McKinneys' garden. Luckily, no one was outside. I snuck to the back door and peered into the window. The kitchen was empty, so I tried the knob. It clicked open. *Thank goodness for country homes.* The room was quiet except for anxious thoughts in my head. I peaked into the empty living room across from me and scurried back into the kitchen. Now to find Auntie, or Auntie's Mutabo. I figured she'd be in the lab but I wanted to make sure the coast was clear. I moved slowly out of the kitchen again. I heard tires on pavement and hid posthaste. I held my breath listening to the sounds of a car door shutting. My heart was pounding. My Dad came through the front doors and I thought he'd walked all the way past. I creeped out thinking I'd just missed him. I hadn't.

He shouted, "Juniper!"

I backed away as if I could retroactively hide myself. I wracked my brain for an explanation.

"What are you doing here?" He asked.

I stood there, motionless and starting to sweat, "Dad, I'm sorry. I really had to get back. I'm so sorry."

"How did you even get back here? I left you with your mother."

"I had a cab bring me. I paid them!" I lied.

I was getting uncomfortably good with lies.

"I'm sorry," I said almost in a whisper.

I wanted to blurt out the truth to him then more than ever. I needed him to know I wasn't just being a horrible daughter. There was a method to my madness, or at least I hoped.

"I'm sorry I snuck out. I know I've been weird lately. I'm here because there's something I have to do. Dad, you've gotta trust me on this," I said with pleading eyes.

The tears in my eyes said more than I could out loud. He scratched his head and chuckled. The sort of chuckle that's more like a question mark than a laugh.

"You are something else, you know that?"

I let myself breathe again. I hugged him as tightly as I could and said nothing else. I'd already said enough.

"Hey, don't get too excited," He spoke more seriously now. "I'm sure your mother's realized you're gone by now. I'll talk to her, but we will deal with it later. You'll leave with me, you hear me?"

I nodded and hugged him again.

I spied on Dad from the stairs, as he spoke with Auntie's Mutabo in the living room. I knew it was the creature by the coldness in its voice. Auntie would never look so icy. They were arguing about something lab-related again, but I didn't have enough information to put the pieces together.

Dad's nose flared in anger. Auntie raised her voice, though each talked over the other, slinging blame. There was something about the serum getting misplaced and

Uncle finding it again. Auntie's Mutabo was defensive and Dad utterly distressed. I feared it wasn't much longer before the Mutabo used more than just its words to try to intimidate my dad. I made my way toward the basement. Now was a better time than ever to see what I could find in the lab.

I was so focused I didn't see Uncle Robbie walking down the hallway toward me.

"Hey, Uncle Robbie!"

I kept moving, veering only slightly to avoid him before he could respond. I raced down the basement stairs to the lab. I shut the door quietly behind me. The lab was sterile and white. Glassware and tubing sat on meticulously organized metal shelves. The stainless steel countertops were spotless, except for Valeferus plants and a few vials. The back wall was bulging with field data, graphs, slides, and photos, all the things Bree and I had helped with on the site. The floor was gray concrete and clean as it could be. Everything seemed to have its exact place, but no serum to be found.

I opened heavy steel cabinets only to find flowers, some dried, others crushed into powders or with their components isolated into various vials. Another cabinet only held a few manila folders. I was running out of places to look.

I heard someone walking above me and crouched behind the island. Maybe it was Uncle Robbie confused. I hoped with everything that it was. The walking stopped. I heard the faint noise of conversation, then the basement door opened. I peeked around the edge of the island. Someone was coming down the stairs.

I scooted around the corner of the island wall, coordinating my movement so I wouldn't be seen. One second of hesitation would have been disaster. I hid between a tall plant and a cardboard box full of broken tubes.

Mutabo and Dad opened the basement door and went straight to the island counter. Auntie's Mutabo pulled out a tiny vial from its pocket and dangled it unsuspectingly under a light.

"Well, what about the old samples? The ones from a month ago?" Dad asked.

"No. Nothing. Actually, I think we should go back to the site. None of these are working how we suspected. We should probably throw this one away, to be honest."

The Mutabo clicked the serum on the island, the flat sound of metal and glass making me jump.

"Wow . . . This just doesn't make any sense. Are you sure?" Dad asked.

The Mutabo clapped him on the back, false concern coating from every word as it said, "We'll figure it out, I'm sure. We've just gotta put those missing pieces together."

"Hmm," Dad scratched his head.

"How about we leave this here overnight and think about it tomorrow? We've been at this for so long, maybe we just need a breather."

After a heavy pause my Dad nodded and they walked out the basement back up the stairs.

Now I knew my dad's serum was complete. There's no way my dad would think it was ready when it actually wasn't. Not the guy who's been conducting scientific experiments since grade school with thorough dedication.

I got up as soon as I heard them close the basement door. My heart pounded, it felt like it was going to burst through my skin, as I grabbed the green liquid off the counter.

The door squeaked, the hinges plaintive as it swung wide. Panicking, I only had time to hide the serum, but not myself. I stood there with my hands behind my back, in plain sight when the Mutabo entered.

"What are you doing?" It barked.

"Uh . . . Well, I've always wanted to see the lab, so…" I stuttered.

Its eyes narrowed to slits. It was eerie watching Auntie's face contort in such unfamiliar ways. It scanned me and leaned in uncomfortably close.

The Mutabo looked me square in my eyes, and through a smile that more closely resembled the bearing of teeth said, "If you wanted a tour, you could have just asked."

I shuddered inside.

Still, I tried to hide how creeped out I was, "Oh, great! I mean, sure. But actually right now, I'm gonna find Bree, so maybe a little later?"

I tried to walk past, but it latched onto my arm.

"You think you're clever," its stiff grip tightened.

I tore away and ran upstairs. I had a one-track mind: get to Bree. I didn't have time to waste.

I raced up to Bree's room, but she wasn't there. The sun was about to set, which meant I had about ten minutes of Earth time to find her.

My dad met me at the front door, "You ready to go?"

"One second!" I shouted, as I darted past him to the backyard.

I ran past the pigs and horses, and I didn't see her anywhere. The only other place she could be was the garden, and I wished with all of my being I'd find her there. I stood before the fountain, frantically looking around, hoping she was nearby. No luck.

I turned, ready to race back into the house one more time and slammed into the Mutabo.

"Give it to me." It hissed.

I clutched the vial deep inside my pocket.

"Where's Bree? What did you do to her?" I demanded.

"Bree's safe and sound. Something I can't say for you right now."

Safe and sound. I knew that meant the opposite. I broke out in a cold sweat.

"Now, just give me the serum, and you'll stay safe, too. Promise."

I bluffed, "Tell me where she is, and I'll give it to you."

I took the serum out of my pocket and held it in front of its face.

"Fair enough."

Its eyes darted to my hand, and it leaned in to swipe the vial, but I jerked it away. The Mutabo puffed its chest and stared down at me with icy eyes. If I tried to run, it would catch me. If I stayed in place for too long, it'd find a way to reach me. I took a quick step forward and kicked the side of its knee with everything I had, and I broke its stance. It tried to wrap its arms around me to bring me down but I stepped back in time.

I made a break for the fountain. I heard the Mutabo scramble to its feet and career after me. When I looked back, it was close, but not close enough.

"C'mon!" I panicked, with no sign of the portal the closer I got to the fountain.

It was too late to wait for Bree. The Mutabo caught up to me. I fought it back with one hand and began to try and hold the vial out of its reach.

As we struggled, the portal began to bloom. We were both consumed by the vortex, paralyzed by the timeless space, but it held on to me nonetheless. The hole of the vortex opened and spat us out onto the lavender shore. The plum waves roared, and bright blue rain fell from the sky in furious sheets.

When I found my footing, I sprang up, brushing my hair out of my face as I glanced around and saw more Mutabo and Beyans in the distance.

The Mutabo had returned to its original form and had fallen backwards. While it struggled to catch its breath, I pulled the bottle swiftly out of its reach and ran.

"It doesn't matter what you do. I will catch you!" It screamed, its panting voice barely audible over the rain.

I knew I had a few moments before it gained enough strength after stealing my Auntie's body for so long.

Adrenaline washed all through me like lightning. My mind was moving too quickly for my body to respond. I tripped over a rock, and my leg gave out. It was only a few seconds, but the hesitation haunted me. It was right behind me. I thought as quickly as I could.

There has to be something—

Out of the corner of my eye, scattered and half buried in the sand, I saw broken swords, spears, and arrows—leftovers from the battle drifting across the beach.

Behind me, the Mutabo closed the distance between us once more and crowed, "You're not so clever after all." It bunched the collar of my shirt in its fist and began to lift me to my feet.

"I've killed much bigger creatures than you!" The Mutabo sneered, and I knew that was true, but I was too determined to be afraid.

I drove the jagged remnants of a sword deep into the top of its thigh with every bit of my strength. Its grey blood reminded me of lava. It stumbled to the ground, dropping me.

"Did you think you were going to get off that easy, Mutabo?" I jibed, all out of breath.

I scrambled out of its reach, "Besides, you talk too much."

I kicked it in the injured thigh. I still had one goal, so I asked, "Where is Bree? Where is Auntie Elaine? *Where are they?*"

The Mutabo's face was pinched with pain, but defiant. I picked up the long half of a broken spear and held it against its chest.

"You wouldn't." It laughed maniacally.

I doubted myself briefly, too, but people were counting on me. People I had begun to care about when I never thought I would.

"Try me."

I pressed the spearhead into his ribs. The sky continued to pour around us, and the battle raged on in the distance, but I kept my gaze on that thing. A small drop of grey black blood emerged where I pressed into its ribs.

Wincing, it said, "Fine! Fine. I put Bree in a cave by the east shoreline, in your city."

There was no way I could return to her in North Carolina *and* deliver the serum in time.

"And Auntie!" I screamed.

"Mutabo territory."

I pressed the spear harder. Its eyes bulged.

"Hey! I've got nothin' to do with that!"

"All of the Mutabo are here, in Cantatis?"

"Yes! With Malum of the Mutabo. He is our leader."

I had to make a choice. I hoped Bree wouldn't hate me for it. I hoped I could do it without her. The Mutabo before me laid there starting to shake. I put the serum back in my pocket and left the creature lying there like the loser it was. I sludged through clingy sand on my way to the Mutabo's lair.

The fight in front of me got clearer with every step. As I got closer I thought I was imagining it when I saw Bree in the distance. *No way.*

Bree charged towards me in battered armour, a glowing sword in her hand, warding off Mutabo until she go to me, "June!"

More than the sight of her wounds, I didn't know what to think about her being there.

I threw my arms around her, hugging her as tightly as I could over her clunky armor. "Oh my god! How did you get here, I thought you were—"

"I was. The spirit guides helped me get here. Long story."

"It's okay, tell me later! We have to get to Mutabo territory somehow and find your mom! Now!"

Bree nodded pointing into the forest, "I've seen some wounded ones making their way that direction. It has to be there."

Bree led us to the lair in a sprint we both knew could be our last.

CHAPTER SIXTEEN

Without having a formal plan, we snuck up to the cave's entryway. It looked to me like no one was guarding it. All I was sure of was that we had to find the real Auntie Elaine, and take down Malum.

Inside, the cave was dimly lit, and the sound of droplets and slick stone ground hailed under our feet. I had to step carefully, because there were abandoned weapons strewn all around us. I picked up a sword and gripped it tightly as we continued. It was obvious that a battle had raged here not too long ago.

I heard voices ahead of us and saw wavering light from a torch.

"When should we kill the human?" one voice asked.

I held my breath, because we both knew what they meant by "human." We waited for the light to disappear deeper in the cave and the voices to silence before we trailed them. I was cold, but sweat still permeated my clothes.

We reached a spiral staircase more brightly lit by torches. We crept down deeper into the lair. The corridors seemed to echo Mutabo laughter from no discernable direction. It grew, escalating as we inched closer to the heart of their base. My breathing came loud and ragged, and sweat seemed to gush out of my pores. I was certain we were getting close.

Bree's eyes locked on mine, one of the only times I had ever seen her so serious, and she said, "This is it."

The first several doors led to giant, empty rooms. As we searched, the laughter seemed to grow and fade, not at all helping us gauge our proximity to Malum. Then for a long while, it was just corridors and stairs leading down deeper into their lair.

After we'd gone down three different flights, we rounded one more corner with magnificently carved doors that were open just slightly. We exchanged stares, before gradually pushing them open. On the other side was a room full of Mutabo.

"Get down!" I hissed, and we backed into a shadowy corner.

Aggro had told us Mutabo couldn't see very well, but I wasn't about to take a chance. Bree tucked her sword in her belt loop.

The giant oxen-like creatures sat at long tables covered in elaborate displays of bread, fruits, meats, and wine. The floors were covered in glass and trash. At the front of the room, performing for an inattentive Malum, was a nervous fairy, hurriedly flying and flitting in the air to everyone else's apparent joy. Malum was larger than the rest and more colorful, with a yellow and orange chest and horns wrapped in a metal crown.

In the dark corners of the hall, there were small caged-in rooms filled with sort of zombie-like holograms of humans, as if their souls had been put behind bars. Well, all were holographic except one, Auntie Elaine, who pulled frantically at the bars to get out.

"Mom," Bree whispered. Her grip tightened on her sword. My pace was careful and slow as I began to move.

"I'll go first." I took a deep breath to steady myself and slinked slowly along the edge of the floor, stopping in a dark corner closer to the steps leading to the prisoners above us.

Come on, I mouthed, eyes wide. Too late. Bree's sword disappeared in her hand and she began to crawl. In slow motion, I watched as her foot crunched on glass making a devastating crunch that somehow echoed in the hall. Bree kept moving like nothing happened, but surely everyone knew something had. The creatures fell into whispers, as they looked around, swiveling their giant heads in complete silence.

"A human!" one shouted, pointing right at Bree.

I crawled out of my corner exposing myself.

"So good to have new friends!" Malum sneered. "Let's show our guests how we entertain humans here, shall we?"

A Mutabo grabbed me. Bree somehow broke away from another Mutabo's grasp and tried to save me, but she couldn't.

"Well done! Well done!" Malum cheered.

He stood and began to walk toward us. I shuddered. He had to be at least nine feet tall, his pointy feet scraping on the stone.

"You must be the new lot. See we got some little ones this time, eh?"

His minions laughed uproariously. I couldn't move much, but I struggled against the hold of the strong Mutabo.

"You. What's your name?" He gripped my chin in one hand.

"None of your business," I yanked my face away from him, leaving a stinging scratch from his nail.

"This one's feisty!" He jeered, "I love to know the names of my victims. Intruders like yourselves give us a good reason to have a fire show. Nothin' chars quite so nicely as feisty human flesh."

The room erupted with hearty cheers.

My arm was starting to burn from the Mutabo's iron grasp.

"Let us go, or I promise you'll be sorry!" Bree threatened.

But Malum and the others only laughed.

"How exciting. Lock em' up for safe keeping. I've had a hard couple of days. This will be a nice reward. And get that fire room ready."

He stared right at me when he said "fire room." I stared back, as the Mutabo dragged us into the prison beside Auntie's. The Mutabo shouted back at Auntie,

"Enough out of you!"

Auntie's protests grew to whispers. The Mutabo continued.

"Let's get the fairy over here and mute this one." I watched as the fairy reluctantly flew up to Auntie's cell and threw up both of her hands. Two light beams floated into Auntie's cell and she went silent. Bree began to yell but I hushed her, afraid we'd get the same treatment. The fairy flew back down and began to perform again as if she never stopped, with a numb expression on her face. There was a small opening connecting us to into Auntie's space, only big enough for me to reach through and Auntie reached out to us. Bree grabbed her hand tight. I paced around in the prison unsure of what to do. After more celebration and eating Malum left with several guards following close behind him, and the space grew strangely calm.

The remaining Mutabo left too, until there were only two guards downstairs, glancing up every so often, but not a lot. Eventually, they fell asleep at their posts, snoring as they leaned against the stone walls.

As soon as they snored, Bree nudged me as I'd been sitting and so I stood.

"I grabbed this when we were fighting. I couldn't say anything, but this has to be our way out."
She held up a small bundle of keys like they'd unlock the secrets of life, which wasn't too far off from what we were dealing with. She unlocked us first, then Auntie, and their embrace made me want to cry. Not just because it was beautiful, but because I didn't notice how afraid I was until that moment. I swished the serum around in my pocket. I had to remind myself why I was there. I simmered on what we should do next. Auntie opened her mouth to speak and mouthed words but nothing came out. She was distraught and panicked silently.

"Mom, it's okay, we're going to get you out of here." Bree promised.
Bree looked to me and I knew then I couldn't leave with them but I didn't want to say it out loud, because that would make it real.

I took a deep breath, then spoke, "Bree, I need you to lead your mom out to safety. I've gotta hang back—"

"June, I'm supposed to be your partner in this. I can't just leave you by yourself." She protested.

If Auntie had a voice I knew she'd be yelling at us. She folded her arms and shook her head and motioned as if to say, "What the hell is happening?"

"You're not just leaving me, Bree. The best way for you to help us win this thing is get your mother to safety. I can handle everything else. You have to trust me on this." I said as assertively as I felt.

Bree turned to her mother and said,

"Mom we'll be okay so soon, I promise. I promise you."

She hugged her mother whose face was filled with confusion and distress.

"Bree, I need you to find Aggro. Bring your mother there. I'll fight Malum."

Bree nodded.

Auntie looked to have had accepted she'd have to listen to me.

Bree asked me with what, and I told her myself. I acted brave but I was very afraid, as I watched Bree lead Auntie away.

The guards behind us ruffled in their sleep. I didn't have much time. I whispered to the elders to have my back. I hoped they were listening.

I flattened myself around each corner and down the stairs after Bree. I tiptoed past sleeping guards into a dimly lit hallway, and I could only see a few feet in front of me at any moment. Creatures spoke not too far from where I walked. I hid in a dip in the hallway to listen.

Two higher-pitched voices spoke about the battle supplies, their boots strong, surefooted in the dark. I followed the sound of their voices through the corridors as far as I was able, while still keeping a safe distance. My instincts told me Malum would be nearby.

One of the first voices said, "Lord Malum's preparing now. He will roast those humans tonight, you know."

I shuddered.

"That'll be festive, for sure!" the other cheered.

I waited for them to pass the room I suspected to be Malum's. He sang from his room in a deep, raspy voice, something about killing us all. I wasn't impressed. But I was scared. I knew I shouldn't be, I couldn't be, but I was.

I took a long, deep breath just for me and opened the door without giving myself a moment to change my mind. The room was huge, and he was on the other side. He kept singing, not even noticing me.

"You tiptoe as if I couldn't hear you." He turned to me smirking.

I stood much stronger than I felt and demanded, "I'm not afraid of you."

"Stoic, I see." He chuckled, moving a few leisurely paces away from me, unfazed.

I moved even closer to him, standing my ground. He watched me and laughed, patting his knee.

"Humans are such dumb creatures. You pretend to be tough and then you die. You will die, you know, and I'll be the one to kill you."

"You wish." I said, unwavering.

His mockery flipped something in me. My fear was replaced with rage. This was the monster wanting to kill me, my family, my friends. Wanting to take over my home and the Earth and the world as I knew it. I growled and shook off my doubt. All the anger in me channeled into that moment.

He moved faster than his body made it seem like he could. In an instant, he knocked me over and kicked me to the ground. He towered over me in that gigantic, wood-rich room. I had never felt so small, and as you know, I've felt very small before.

"Well that was no fun. Here, let's try that again."

He handed me a sword from his shelf and stepped back to let me get up. I barely stood before he kicked me down again. My back throbbed in pain.

"You don't scare me!" I yelled. I wasn't lying.

"Then fight me!" He replied.

I stood up again, this time slowly and painfully.

"You're the one that's afraid of me," I prosed, challenging the beast.

He threw his head back in guffaws of laughter. I let him laugh. He charged towards me and put his large hand around my neck. I was quickly starting to lose my breath. Through staggered breaths I said,

"I'm not afraid of you, you know that. You're trying to hide your fear."

He grunted and threw me by my neck to the ground. I was in too much pain to get up. I gasped for air.

"You talk too much. You must want a painful death."

I struggled to stand. Once I had my footing again I said, "You're afraid of powers you didn't even know I had!" I was starting to feel stronger again.

I spoke louder, "You're afraid that I will make you small! As small as you are inside!"

He was still laughing, but right in front of me, he shrank. I couldn't just be seeing things. He was smaller than he was only seconds ago, if only by a little. He charged towards me again and knocked me to the ground. Pain bloomed in my side. I kept speaking.

"You're nothing but a joke. A joke who I will defeat, and then you will be nothing!" His laughter faded, and he picked up a knife from a table beside him.

"You are nothing!" I yelled from the ground. I pulled myself up again.

I spoke with every bit of intention. I didn't let his newfound weapon scare me.

"You are nothing, and you've never been anything. This war will end with you begging me to pity you."

He shrank. More and more, he shrank right before my eyes. His eyes grew big with fear. He watched his hands shrink, and I could smell the fear floating off of him and enveloping the room. The smaller he got, the closer I came, and the less my heart pounded.

"You're shrinking. Don't you see you're going to lose? You and your army will never take over Earth. Not with me protecting it.!"

I didn't even need to yell anymore. I felt powerful. I spoke almost in a whisper, watching this once nine-foot-tall giant disappear in its clothes. He yelled up at me, and I could barely hear the voice coming out of this now gerbil-sized character.

"You'll never win!" he said.

And this time it was my turn to laugh.

"I already have."

I picked up Malum and watched him disappear in the palm of my hands. I surveyed the now quiet room. Nothing, no one. Just me and the clothes of a once-powerful creature. I stared at the clothes on the ground and watched the ground beneath me shake. Wind swirled around me and in front of me appeared a familiar face. My grandmother. Her smile was vibrant and kind and she nodded at me. I felt a calm rush over me.

"Grandma." I said. Not to call after her or ask her to stay, but simply to acknowledge her presence. She was with me. She always was. She slowly faded in front of me and I was left with the calming quiet of the room. I smiled to myself.

It's like seeing her was a key unlocking all of the anger and resentment I held for my grandmother leaving me alone. A weight was lifted. I was free.

The halls of the cave castle were silent. Giant garments of clothes cluttered the halls where Mutabo used to be. I ran to the empty celebration hall, where the clothes of the guards lay next to the doors. The cages that once held the holograms of humans were gone.

Someone shouted behind me, "Juniper!"

It was Bree.

"What happened? They all disappeared! What the fuck?"

She would never believe how we won.

"Well done," Harmonia bowed to us.

Aggro and all the other fairies behind Harmonia did, too. I brushed off my tattered clothes and stood proudly beside Bree. Auntie was long ago at home safe with her memory washed by Harmonia.

Bree later told me about how she'd made it back to Cantatis without me. She'd fought two disguised Mutabo in human police bodies. She made them release her out of the prison Auntie's Mutabo had put her in and lead her to Cantatis.

"Bree. You are fearless, strong, and loyal. You are a born warrior. Thank you for your service. And Juniper.

Your grandmother would be so proud. You are more like her than you realize."

"The two of you make a great team," Aggro added.

He was right, we did make a good team. Bree squeezed my hand.

Harmonia sent us off with a few last words, "Until we meet again."

A light flashed, and Bree and I fell into Bree's room. We jumped up and hugged each other. My Dad called eventually called up and I begged for more time and we stayed up as long as we could. That is, until I heard a familiar voice call from downstairs. My mother.

I looked at Bree and she told me, "Go."

The first thing I did when I reached her was say, "I'm sorry. For everything."

We stared at each other, and both started to tear up.

All of a sudden I was blubbering.

We were both blubbering. It was a cry so necessary, so long-awaited, that it felt like laughter. She held me close, and we did what we should have done months ago. She told me Grandma would have laughed about my thinking going out to a club would be "grown up." I told her I know, and she told me not to get ahead of myself.

"Ma would have gotten a kick out of this trip." She laughed.

She said that I was still on punishment when we got back home. I figured as much. When we were done talking, we wiped our eyes, and Mom lead me to the kitchen.

We were met there by Uncle Robbie, holding a cake with *Happy Birthday Juniper!* written under buttercream juniper leaves. Behind him was my dad, Auntie, and Robbie Jr.

Turns out Bree and my parents talked that morning and had decided to keep the party on. My mom had told them I would learn my lesson in time for a celebration. If only they knew how much it took me to get there.

While eating my cake, a couple neighbors I hadn't met yet arrived. They wished me a happy sweet sixteen and gave me the best gifts: money.

I stepped outside for a bit to get some air.

Bree followed, "So, I brought you a lil' something for the day, too."

She wore her signature smirk.

"What's that? I asked.

"Ok, so I know we, like, didn't really get along for a minute."

"A minute?" I laughed. We both did.

"Listen! Ok, so I know we didn't get along for *a while* but you're low key my closest friend now, so I wanted to do something cool for you on your birthday."

My heart smiled.

"I'm your closest friend now? I asked.

She nodded.

"You're mine, too." I said, and I meant it. I never thought that's something I would say to Bree McKinney, that's for sure.

Bree went on,

"Ok, now close your eyes. Close em'!" She shouted, before pulling me into the garden. Finally she instructed me to open my eyes.

Sen.

"Happy birthday, Juniper."

Sen was standing there with her gorgeous smile and a card in her hand. Bree skipped off, like the mischievous girl I never thought I'd call a friend three months ago, and I loved her for it.

Sen led me out of the garden and away from all the houseguests to the pigsty.

Wilbur stared at us, and I said, "Let's move over here," pointing towards the shed.

I didn't want a talking pig to watch our intimate moment.

"Uh, okay," Sen laughed.

"Sen, I'm so, so sorry for throwing up in you. I'm never drinking again, seriously. I'm so sorry."

She shook her head and said, "It's okay, it was actually pretty funny after I thought about it. Plus now you've got your wild story."

We laughed, remembering our conversation weeks ago.

Our giggling faded, until we were just looking at each other. My cheeks got hot and palms sweaty for all the best reasons. Sen leaned in, in spite of my sweaty palms and hot cheeks, and she kissed me. She *kissed* me.

"Wow," was all I could think to say.

The card in her hand was her confession that she had a crush on me the entire summer. She gave me her email so we could stay in touch when I got back to Hamilton. I promised to email her as soon as I got home. When I checked my home computer, she'd already written to me. *I can't wait to go on a real date with you.* She wrote.

I responded within minutes of dropping my luggage, *I've been wanting to tell you the same thing!*

Bree and I agreed to meet up via teleporting, until Bree saved up to officially come visit me back home in a way we could actually tell our parents about. We're already planning our trip to London, since that didn't go so smoothly the first time.

And as for Cantatis, that was only the beginning, or at least I think so. Aggro told us we still had a lot of training to do, so we'd be seeing them soon. Next time around, I am ready for whatever shenanigans they have for me.

I'll never forget my three months in North Carolina. I don't know what's to come, but right now, in this moment, I'm not afraid. I am the granddaughter of Alice Jackson, an Ambassador of this great Earth, and I know with all my heart she's proud of me. I know somewhere down the road I'll meet a challenge and be scared out of my mind, but please, Journal, when that happens, you'll have to remind me to be fearless. Remind me of the wild story about the time I saved the world.

ACKNOWLEDGMENTS

Thank you to my partner and love Cassia for believing in me when I definitely wasn't believing in myself. I should note, if it wasn't for Cassia's many edits and keen eye for detail, I highly doubt I'd be as proud of *Juniper Leaves* as I am. Thank you to my big sister Jessica, who used her phenomenal teaching skills to read, reread and read again every single draft of *Juniper Leaves*. Thank you to my mom Joanne Joyner for teaching me to dream. Who else do you think I get these fantastical ideas from? Thank you to my sister Jalisa and Michael Bennett for creating such an amazing cover. Also, to Aspen Aten for the former and OG book cover that holds a very special place in my heart. Thank you to the small publishing company that I shall not name (for legal reasons) that rightfully dropped my project because it just wasn't ready. You pushed me to make my work better and it would not be what it is today without your difficult decision. And finally, thank you so, so much to each and every one of my Kickstarter supporters who made *Juniper Leaves* a successful campaign, especially to Amika Cooper, Caleb H. Bercu, Mariel Simmonds-Little, Renee Miller, and my aunt Patrice Joyner who went above and beyond in your donations. So many of you have reached out over these many months (ok, years) about what progress I've made and I'm truly thankful for your patience as I struggled to complete this project.

Jaz Joyner